DEVILS' SPAWN

CHARLES LLOYD BIRKIN was born in England in 1907 and was educated at Eton College from 1921-1926. His contributions to British horror began in 1932 when publisher Philip Allan employed him to edit the *Creeps* series of short story collections, which included volumes with titles like *Creeps, Shudders, Shivers, Nightmares, Tales of Death,* and *Tales of Fear.* The books, with their sensational dust jacket art and stories by an impressive list of writers that included H.R. Wakefield, Lord Dunsany, Russell Thorndike, and Birkin himself (under the name Charles Lloyd), are highly collectible today and were the precursors of later popular British horror anthologies, such as the *Pan Books of Horror Stories.* Birkin's contributions to the *Creeps* volumes were collected in his first book, *Devils' Spawn* (1936), the only book published by Birkin before a long hiatus. In 1942, he succeeded his uncle as the 5th Baronet Birkin, and he served in the Second World War in the Sherwood Foresters.

Following a long break, Birkin resumed writing after his return to London in 1960 and, perhaps at the instigation of Dennis Wheatley, began publishing new collections of short stories with *The Kiss of Death* (1964), for which Wheatley provided an introduction. Several more volumes of tales appeared between 1965 and 1970, including *The Smell of Evil* (1965), also introduced by Wheatley. From 1970 to 1974 Birkin lived in Cyprus, which he fled in the wake of the Turkish invasion. He and his wife Janet spent their later years in the Isle of Man, where Birkin died in 1985.

By Charles Birkin

★ Published by Valancourt Books

DEVILS' SPAWN

CHARLES BIRKIN

VALANCOURT BOOKS

Devils' Spawn by Charles Birkin
Originally published in Great Britain by Philip Allan in 1936
First American edition published by Valancourt Books in 2015
Published simultaneously in hardcover and paperback

Published by Valancourt Books, Richmond, Virginia
http://www.valancourtbooks.com

ISBN 978-1-943910-13-7 (hardcover)
ISBN 978-1-943910-14-4 (paperback)
Also available as an electronic book.

All Valancourt Books publications are printed on acid free paper that meets all ANSI standards for archival quality paper.

The Publisher is grateful to Mark Terry of Facsimile Dust Jackets, LLC for providing a scan of the dust jacket of the first edition.

Set in Dante MT

CONTENTS

To
WAVERNEY
for her
"ELOEE"

DEVILS' SPAWN

OLD MRS. STRATHERS

She sat in the rocking-chair before the grate of smouldering coal-dust, pressed and damped into a semi-solid mass so that it should burn the longer. Her eyes were bright with a quick nervous light that contrasted forcibly with the monstrous wreck of her face. For when the second stroke had fallen upon her two years previously, not only had all power of movement been taken from her, but she had also lost her power of speech, and was forced to live on, a powerless lump of suffering flesh, twisted and broken. Her body was shapeless in the many shawls that encumbered it. A tattered rug was wrapped round her knees in an endeavour to provide a slight protection against the chill of the poorly heated room.

Old Mrs. Strathers looked at the clock that ticked loudly on the mantelpiece, overcrowded with the ornaments and photographs so dear to her daughter-in-law's heart. She peered into the greyling dusk. Six o'clock. Ronnie should be back soon.

Dear Ronnie! He was the one solace of her mockery of life, devoting himself to her on every possible occasion. But naturally it was only in the early morning and the evening that he could be with her. His office hours were long. Half-past eight until half-past six, with an hour off in the middle of the day. He was working too hard; and he hadn't got the strength to stand it. Molly should have noticed it long since; and made him see a doctor. But no, the poor boy had grown to look worse and worse, until he was little better than a ghost; and it was not until the previous week that he had consulted a doctor—Doctor Hallam, who lived at the end of the street. Old Mrs. Strathers had never felt much confidence in *him*. Careless, and too fond of the bottle, in her opinion. Ronnie hadn't told her very much of what he had said to him. She thought that he had made too light of it all, but that, no doubt, was because he was afraid of alarming her.

Eventually, the head clerk had told him he must seek medical advice; Mrs. Strathers remembered Ronnie telling Molly so. And she, his mother, was powerless to help him.

She looked at the clock. A quarter-past six. What could the boy be doing?

Flanking the clock on either side were two photographs in imitation silver frames. One of Frank, her second husband, dead these fifteen years; and one of her step-son, Charlie. Charlie was a chemist's assistant in the High Street; and doing very well, so she'd been told. She slanted her eyes to the right, and could just see the coloured photograph of Molly, taken when she was engaged to Ronnie. It showed her with her head and shoulders bare, save for a wisp of tulle. Molly thought it very classy.

Old Mrs. Strathers sighed. Ronnie was such a dear sweet boy. She had been against his marriage from the first. A mother always knew when her son was marrying the wrong girl. And she had been right. She knew well enough that Molly and Charlie were carrying on—and they knew that she knew. And that was why they hated her so bitterly.

She heard a key in the lock of the front door. Ronnie, at last.

"Hello, Mother." He came over to her chair and kissed her. "How are you feeling to-night, darling? Is there anything you want?"

They had an arrangement that if Mrs. Strathers was in need of something she should blink her eyes twice.

She tried to smile at him, but was unable to move her contorted mouth. Her eyes, alone, had a brighter light by which she showed her pleasure.

"No, dear?"

He sat down in the chair next to her, and lit a cigarette.

"I get my holiday at the end of the month—and then we can be together for two whole weeks. You'll like that, won't you, mother?"

He always told her of the daily events, and his future plans. He smiled at her.

"Molly's not in yet, I see."

Old Mrs. Strathers looked at his delicate hands. His sunken cheeks, marked with a hectic flush. His blue suit was neat, but much worn and very shiny at the knees and elbows. Molly, she knew, took every penny he made and yet was always in debt. Mrs. Strathers' eyes grew hard as she thought of Molly. Taking Ronnie's money, and living with Charlie under her very eyes! If she'd been Ronnie she'd have turned them both out of the house long ago. But Ronnie would never do that. He was staying here for her sake. He was too poor to support two homes, and it would mean the workhouse for her. The workhouse—that had been her spectre all her life.

Ronnie got up and walked into the kitchen. Soon he came back, a glass in his hand, a glass filled with a pink effervescent fluid.

"I haven't forgotten my tonic to-night, you see!"

He swallowed it at a draught.

"Shall I make you a cup of tea, mother?"

Mrs. Strathers blinked twice. Ronnie was good to her. She was lucky to have such a son. She drank the tea that he held to her mouth greedily. It was her first nourishment since Ronnie had given her her breakfast before he went to the office. Molly had gone out at mid-day and hadn't been back since. Yes—she was indeed lucky to have Ronnie to take care of her.

Old Mrs. Strathers listened intently. The door that led to the steep staircase was ajar. From time to time she could hear low laughter. But there had been silence for a considerable time, now. Charlie had come in about two o'clock. Molly was in the kitchen washing up the dirty plates from the morning's breakfast. Her sleeves were rolled above the elbows of her wet red arms. Charlie had gone straight to the kitchen. There had been the sound of a faint scuffle.

"No, Charlie, don't! Not now! Oh, you are a one!"

Then she had heard them kissing.

"Shut the door—do. *She'll* hear."

"What if she does? *She* can't split on us!"

Charlie had given his coarse loud laugh.

They had stayed in the kitchen quite a while.

"Come on, Molly—leave that till later." Charlie's voice was urgent.

And then they had come into the sitting-room. Molly gave the old woman a look. "You and your Ronnie!" she taunted. "What good is he to a woman like me—eh, Charlie?"

Charlie had made a vulgar noise with his lips, and then they had both gone upstairs.

Old Mrs. Strathers had glared at them defiantly.

What could she do? Oh, what could she do? She thought of them standing there and sneering at her and her boy. Charlie, big and brutal, with his huge body and coarse face. And Molly, pretty still—in her common way. Where was all this leading? What was going to happen?

When Ronnie returned in the evening they had both gone out. He tried to entertain her with his news, but old Mrs. Strathers was inattentive. She *must* think of some way of letting him know what was going on—that his wife was a brazen hussy. A harlot. And they meant him an injury. She was convinced of it.

Ronnie saw that his mother was worried.

"What's the matter, mother? Are you feeling worse to-night? Tell me, what is it?"

He searched her face with his eyes.

"Headache?"

"No?"

"Are you thirsty?"

"Aren't you comfortable?"

But all he could get in reply was the same intent stare. First at the photograph of Molly and then at Charlie's.

"Does Molly want me? Is she ill? Is that what you're trying to tell me?"

In the week that followed, Molly and Charlie treated Mrs. Strathers as if she did not exist. They carried out their love-making openly. She suffered their gibes and taunts, and was spared no humiliation. The climax came two days before Ronnie was due to begin his holiday. Once or twice Molly had noticed Ronnie looking at them curiously, and had surprised Mrs. Strathers giving significant looks, first at their photographs, and then at Ronnie;

and what he had had so much difficulty in understanding was no mystery to her. Something must be done.

That evening when they had finished their supper Charlie said, "Like a cinema, Moll? There's a good one at the Berridge Road."

"Oh, that would be nice. I'd love it. Just a moment while I get my things on."

She got up hastily and ran up the stairs to her room.

And they had gone off.

They were very late in getting back; for after the performance Molly turned to her lover:

"Look here! We've got to talk, I tell you. We've got to *do* something—and do something quick. I've thought of a plan, dear, but I need your help."

"Well, we can't talk here. Come on."

They had walked for an hour, Molly talking eagerly, Charlie answering briefly; occasionally interrupting to ask a question.

When they returned to the house their minds were made up.

If Ronnie died, Molly as his widow would have the house and the furniture. And the old woman? Well, they could fix her all right.

The next evening Molly waited at the corner of the street where Bell and Brown, the chemists in which Charlie worked, was situated. She received many admiring smiles from men who were returning from their work, but she ignored them with exaggerated haughtiness. What could be keeping Charlie? she wondered. She turned and looked at herself in the mirrored walls of the shop-window into which she had been gazing. Smiling ladies of wax postured in peculiar and stilted poses, showing off the "Latest in Lingerie." She pulled her small green hat lower over her eyes and fluffed out the fair hair over her ears. Then she applied her powder puff and lipstick—with more vigour than discretion.

"Hello, Moll. Sorry I'm a bit late. But I had to wait to shut up the shop. Useful that—what?" Charlie laughed, and pulling his tobacco pouch from his pocket, began to stuff his pipe.

"You've got it?"

Molly's voice squeaked nervously in her excitement.

"In here, Love."

He tapped his waistcoat pocket.

"Well, we'd better be getting back, I suppose."

"What's the hurry?"

He bent his head, and shielded the flame of the match. Over his pipe a look of understanding passed between them. She took his arm and together they mingled with the crowds on the pavement—a couple such as can be seen in their hundreds in any big town. Molly—pretty, cheaply but elaborately dressed; artificial silk stockings, high-heeled shoes, short skirt, gay pullover and "novelty" jewellery. Charlie with a bowler hat tipped at a rakish angle, brown suit, an impressive watch-chain from which dangled various charms and seals, and the swagger of a lady-killer.

But there the resemblance to their fellows ended, for there was murder in their hearts. Cold, calculating murder.

Mrs. Medlicott stood in front of the mantelpiece talking to, or, it would be correct to say, talking at, Mrs. Strathers. Her hands were on her hips, her pale eyes alight with interest in what she was saying. She enjoyed talking to Mrs. Strathers. At least, as she was constantly telling her husband, the old woman was a good listener.

". . . And there she was, beating on the door. But her mother wouldn't let her in, and quite right too, I says." She finished with unctuous relish.

Old Mrs. Strathers fixed her eyes politely on her visitor.

"But I really must be going. It's nearly time for Tim's tea," Mrs. Medlicott continued. "And by the way, I *was* sorry to hear that Ronnie's been badly. Such a good boy, Tim and I have always thought, and such a good son, too! I hope that Mrs. Ronnie appreciates him as much as others do."

There was a malicious thrust in this last statement, since Molly's "flightiness" was common knowledge in the street.

"It's his heart, I suppose. . . . I once had an uncle, poor man, who was took just the same way. He dropped down dead all of a sudden, one day. But then we've all got to die some day—it's a short life but a gay one." And with this singularly inapt observation Mrs. Medlicott patted her hostess on the shoulder, and went off to her own home, firmly convinced that she had been very charitable in cheering up "that poor old thing at Number Eight."

But in spite of everything Mrs. Strathers was happier than she had been for a long time; for Ronnie's holiday began on the following day, and she would have him with her all the time for the next two weeks.

Molly found it very difficult during the succeeding days to keep the excitement from her face. That the old woman suspected something she was certain. Her eyes never left Ronnie's figure, unless to follow Charlie, or to watch with eager interest Molly's every movement.

And so it was not until the following Monday evening that Molly found the opportunity for which she had waited. Charlie had gone to play billiards; and Ronnie was out for a short walk. It was seven o'clock. Molly had noticed that usually he took his tonic at a quarter past.

The sitting-room was empty save for Mrs. Strathers—watchful and alert.

Molly crossed to the shelf where the bottle stood, and emptied into it the contents of a tiny cardboard box she carried in her hand. A few of the crystals fell on to the shelf. Carefully she brushed them back into the box. She looked at the back of the chair where old Mrs. Strathers sat. She couldn't have seen anything. . . . Then her eyes travelled past the old woman hunched in her chair, to the ornate mirror that hung above the mantelpiece. Mrs. Strathers was staring back at her with horror and mute rage. She had seen everything. Well—it couldn't be helped.

"So you saw, did you—you old image," Molly cried shrilly. "Thought it might be something to hurt your precious son, eh? You're not far wrong either."

She ran to the old woman's chair and shook her roughly by the shoulder.

"And when he's dead you're going to the workhouse where you should have been long since—with your nosey-parker spying ways."

She broke off as she glanced at the clock. Time she was off!

"See you later—you old idol."

She slammed the street door and hurried away, her high heels tap-tapping on the pavement.

Old Mrs. Strathers waited for Ronnie to come back.

"I've brought you these violets, mother. There was a poor woman selling them in Civiter Street. Look—I'll put them on the mantelpiece, where you can see them."

His mother looked at him fixedly; imploring him to see the urgency of her appeal. Ronnie had his back to her, arranging the flowers in a small bowl of glazed earthenware.

"There!"

He bent down and kissed the top of her head.

"Now we'll have a quiet talk before the others come back—but before I forget, I'll just take my tonic."

He picked up the bottle and measured out a dose.

"Beastly nuisance these hearts, aren't they, darling?"

The muscles in Mrs. Strathers' throat were taut in her effort to speak. Her face was suffused with a deep flush.

Ronnie drained his glass, making a wry face as he did so.

A terrible rasping croak sounded from the old lady's chair.

Ronnie crossed the room in two strides, dropping the glass in his surprise. Splinters of glass sprinkled the linoleum on the floor.

"Mother—what is it?"

And then he felt the pain; at first in red-hot spasms, then more and more frequently.

"Mother—don't be frightened—but—I think—I'm—ill."

Doubled up in agony he clutched the edge of the table. The corner of the cloth was in his hand.

He fell to the floor. There was a crash as the crockery on the table slithered to the linoleum.

Ronnie was gasping; fighting for breath. His lungs laboured in the battle to draw in air. His eyes protruded, the irises turned toward the upper lids. A thick retching battled in his gullet.

He choked, twitched, convulsed with spasms, and lay still.

In the mirror old Mrs. Strathers saw his body, spread-eagled, and half shrouded by the tablecloth.

A quarter of an hour later Molly returned. She glanced quickly round the room, saw Ronnie lying on the floor . . . the splintered glass starring the oilcloth . . . the contorted attitude of the corpse.

For a moment she waited, making sure that nothing had been overlooked. Satisfied, she hurried to the door, and half-staggered into the street.

"Mrs. Medlicott! Mrs. Medlicott!" Her shout echoed down the canyon of the houses. "Mrs. Medlicott . . . come at once . . . Ronnie's been taken badly."

Doors opened and heads were popped out of the windows. Soon a small crowd peered through old Mrs. Strathers' door . . . attracted by the urgency of Molly's cries. The heartless curiosity of the slums, determined to miss no atom of drama. Mrs. Medlicott ran from her house. She found Molly on her knees by Ronnie's body. Instantly, gratified by being the centre of attraction, she gave instruction to the group of spectators.

"Get the ambulance . . . a doctor . . . Hallam from Number Seventy-eight." A boy, eager to be of use, hurried away. "Not that he can be of much use. The poor boy's dead as dead! I had an uncle what was took the same way, poor soul. Heart too, same as this one."

"Percy"—Molly turned to one of the onlookers—"go round to Bell and Brown's, and tell Charlie to come at once . . . there's a good boy."

The crowd outside the door eddied back, to make way for the doctor. Doctor Hallam took in the scene in the little sitting-room . . . noted the twisted position of the body.

"Doctor," Molly was distraught, "I've been afraid of this for a long time. Ronnie has been queer as queer lately . . . and *so depressed*." She got up as the doctor knelt down. There was an interested silence, as he made his swift preliminary examination.

"What is it?" Molly whispered. "Heart failure . . . is he dead?" Doctor Hallam shook his head gravely. Mrs. Medlicott was thrilled.

"Pore thing! . . . Suicide?"

The street considered suicide as a disgrace second only to murder. The doctor made no reply, but turned again to his investigation.

Old Mrs. Strathers sat hunched in her chair, gazing at the heap of smouldering coal-dust. Dimly she heard the buzz of voices;

but they came as if from a great distance. Her eyes were focussed on a bunch of violets in a brown earthenware bowl.

After a time the crowd was dispersed, and Charlie and Molly were left alone with the old woman.

Two days later the authorities sent to take her to the work-house.

The verdict was "Suicide while of unsound mind." Mrs. Medlicott conveyed this information to old Mrs. Strathers on the occasion of the first of her rare visits to the workhouse; but the old woman seemed to have lost all interest in the subject, for she closed her eyes, and refused to open them again until after her visitor had left.

SHELTER

The sky had the appearance of lead; not the greyness that is so often the prelude to a shower, but the hard threatening monotone that, in conjunction with an expectant silence, precedes the breaking of a storm. Anxiously the rider searched for some sign of human habitation, but only the foothills, robbed of colour, stretched in unbroken sequence to the horizon.

Far away a growl of thunder foretold the approach of the tempest. The leaves on the stunted trees whispered of tumult that would shortly lash their branches into a clangour of creaking chaos. The man sat motionless. It would not be a pleasant experience to be overtaken by what he knew was coming; and trees were hardly the ideal protection against the lightning, which, as he looked, rent the heavens, leaving them, by contrast, darker than before, emphasising the dim twilight.

He spoke to his horse. "Come along, old man. If we go on we must get somewhere eventually."

The animal was restless and uneasy. Another growl of thunder followed, more closely this time, by a jagged snake of light.

The track, that until now had been level, began to slant downwards. A gigantic crash, thrown back by the hills, almost deafened the man. The sound, imprisoned among the slopes, muttered in echo. A vicious flash seemed to strike the ground several hundred yards to his right, and still the rain kept off.

Michael Christie patted the frightened horse beneath him. He realised that he was lost. He had set out for Fuiza, planning to stop the night in the hamlet of San Marco.

And then he heard the coming of the rain as it swept through the trees. A large warm drop plashed softly on his upturned face; a second, and the heavy air was cut by the thickening arrows of water. The storm had broken; the lightning and thunder following so closely that they were practically simultaneous; a cannonade of noise and blinding brilliance, making it impossible to see more than a few feet in front of him.

Michael had lived in Brazil some five years and never could he remember a storm of such violence. Praying to what powers there might be for guidance, he battled on. Drenched to the skin, his hands chafed by the wet leather of the reins, his arms aching with the effort of controlling his terrified mount, he covered miles—in what direction he was unable to guess.

Once the horse got away with him, alarmed by an unusually loud thunderclap; and the tired rider was taken unawares. Michael lay along his saddle while saturated branches lashed at him spitefully. His hat had long since been torn from his head by the wind, which had borne it away in triumph; and his fair hair, darkened by the rain, lay plastered to his skull.

With difficulty, and by incredible chance, he regained the track, a muddied river, along which he blundered having no idea of time or distance. In this world of noise and water, this world gone mad, he had ceased to think coherently; there was no use in trying to make for any point, since he had no idea of his whereabouts. The trail descended more steeply. He knew he must be emerging from the hills to the plains. He prayed to God for a sign of shelter. Once he thought he saw a light gleam briefly on the plain below him. A gasp of relief escaped from his lips, but a moment later only the confusing darkness, shattered intermittently by the lightning, remained.

They stumbled down a steep slope, the mud making progress difficult and dangerous. Michael leant back trying to steady the horse in the slippery quagmire. The rain slashed down without mercy.

At last comparatively level ground took the place of the hillside. Tired out, horse and man persevered through the gloom, faintly thinned by the indistinct light of a drowned moon. Michael crouched forward, his head hunched between his heavy shoulders, trying to shield his eyes from the stinging rain. Gradually the storm appeared to be passing; the thunder grew fainter and less frequent; but the downpour pattered on the earth with a settled insistency that spoke of many hours' continuance.

By a fitful gleam of moonlight Michael peered at his watch which he held with clumsy fingers. It pointed to nine o'clock. He could scarcely believe that his battle with the elements had only lasted four hours. A mass of cloud was scudding across the moon, when—glowing in the blackness—in front and to the left of him—Michael saw a square of warm light.

Buoyed up by hope and, at the same time, overcome with fatigue now that a haven was so close at hand, he turned down a narrow lane that led towards what presently he found to be a cluster of farm buildings. Thatched and white-washed barns formed two wings in conjunction with the central house—a low two-storied structure from which gleamed the lighted window that had attracted his attention. He clattered wearily into the yard. The gale screeched round the corners of the dwelling. With an effort he slid from the saddle and stood up to his ankles in the liquid mire. He cupped his hands to his mouth and shouted:

"Hello, there!"

The wind tore the words away and he realised their futility. Leading the horse he walked to the door and beat upon it with his fist. He waited for several minutes, but no one answered his knock. He crossed to the window, but thick curtains of orange-coloured stuff prevented him from seeing into the room. The water dripped from the eaves and gurgled in the gutters in a steady stream. Returning to the door he banged upon it a second time. As, with savage resentment, he was beginning to think that the occupants must be deaf or dead, a man's voice called "Who's there? What do you want?"

"Let me come in. I want shelter," Michael shouted. "I've lost my way. . . . I can't go further to-night."

Cautiously the door was opened a few inches. "Who are you? What do you want?" the voice repeated.

"I'm on my way to Fuiza, and I've lost my way."

The wind and rain swooped against the half-open door, tearing it from the occupant's grasp and sending it clattering back on its hinges against the wall. The man staggered against the strength of the hurricane.

"My horse ... where can I stable it?" Michael bawled, conscious of the other's scrutiny.

"Come, I will show you."

The man struggled to shut the door, and joined Michael in the yard.

"This way. Follow me." He braced himself to the wind.

The horse having been stabled, fed, and rubbed down, Michael followed his host back to the house. In the narrow hall that led into the living-room they studied one another. Michael faced a man of about his own height, dark and handsome and of early middle age. He was dressed in the faded shirt and trousers worn by farmers of the poorer class. His sleeves were rolled to the elbows, displaying muscular forearms covered with thick dark hair. His teeth were very white against a skin of clear olive. In his turn he looked at Michael—at the tall, rather thick figure, the shoulders broad almost beyond proportion; at the blue eyes; the mouth with its sensual lower lip; the wet shirt sticking to the wide, deep chest; at the long legs in their muddied and rain-blackened riding boots.

"You must be tired and hungry," the man said.

He turned as he spoke and led Michael into the living-room, at the end of which a woman was bending over a stove. A rough table was laid for three people. She turned as they entered. Michael saw that she was still young, still in her thirties, and that she had retained the prettiness that often vanished so quickly among her countrywomen.

"My sister Maria . . . Señor . . . ?" The farmer waited for Michael to give his name.

"Christie."

"My name is Lopez," the man added. "The Señor will stay with us to-night."

"The Señor is soaked to the skin," Maria interrupted. "Give him some dry clothes, Pedro, and when he has changed I will have the supper prepared. I will send Dolores with some hot water. Hurry now!"

"Please don't put yourself to so much trouble. If I can have a towel and some dry clothes, really that is all I want," Michael answered. His smile was twisted, and he knew that it was said to be attractive.

He climbed a shallow flight of stairs behind Pedro, and they entered a large and barely furnished room. The farmer put the candle on a shelf by the bed and surveyed his guest.

"We are of a height," he observed. "That is good."

Selecting the necessary garments from a number that hung on pegs behind the door he laid them on a chair.

"When you are ready bring your own clothes with you, and Maria will dry them."

As the door closed Michael breathed a sigh of pleasure. Shelter, warmth and food. He unbuckled his belt, and drew his shirt over his head. The heavy leather boots were difficult to remove owing to the soaking they had received, but at length, after a struggle and much blasphemy, he stood naked, rejoicing in the glow of well-being that followed his vigorous towelling. A few minutes later, dressed in the borrowed clothes, and carrying his own in his arms, he made his way towards the kitchen. An appetising odour rose to greet him. Maria was bustling from her cooking to the table. Rolls of new white bread were beside each plate, and Michael noticed that a fourth had been added. As he reached the bottom of the stairs, a young girl with a shawl wound round her head slipped into the room, shutting the door swiftly behind her.

"That is everything, Dolores?" her mother asked.

"Yes, Mother." The girl removed her shawl and laid it before the stove to dry. She shivered as she said, "Mother of God—the storm is terrible. It frightens me."

"Dolores, we have a guest," Pedro's deep voice broke in.

Michael found his hand holding the girl's; his eyes looking into hers, large and of a soft brown, and fringed with thick lashes that glistened with the rain out of which she had just come.

"You are welcome, Señor."

At supper Michael ate with enormous appetite; his long day in the saddle and the dangers of the storm had tired but not wearied him, and his host was insistent in his attentions. During the meal Michael discussed the farming situation and political topics with Pedro; the women sitting silent. On several occasions, however, Michael surprised them looking at him intently, but on encountering his gaze they appeared confused. He wondered why Maria looked so sad, a covert sadness that she concealed when aware of observation. The farm might be in financial difficulties, Michael thought. The family appeared a united and happy one but . . . one never knew. The older woman, he discovered, was her brother's housekeeper, Pedro being a widower.

While Maria and Dolores cleared away the remains of the supper, Pedro motioned Michael to a chair by the stove and passed him a handful of the native cigarettes, the black tobacco clearly visible through the thin maize paper.

Their task over, the women joined them, Maria with a basket of mending; Dolores sitting with her hands folded in her lap, listening to the talk.

After a time Pedro got out of his chair: "We go to bed early. If you will come with me I will show you to your room."

Obediently Maria crossed to the dresser and brought a candle to her guest. Taking a sliver of wood she thrust it into the stove and set it to the coarse wick.

"Good night, Señor—and may the good God watch over you."

"Good night Señora—and may the blessed Lord protect you."

"Good night, Señor," Dolores half whispered. Her eyes slanted up at him in shy admiration.

Michael followed the farmer to the upper storey; along a white-washed passage, the walls of which were broken in several places by massive doors. As they turned the corner leading to the room allotted to him he fancied that he heard a latch behind him gently drawn to; and idly wondered that he had not heard Maria and Dolores come up—but perhaps a farm-hand also slept in the house. Pedro threw open a door.

"Good night, Señor."

Michael, holding the candle above his head, looked round the room. It was very similar to the one in which he had changed. A vast low bed, a crude dressing-table, and a chair were the only furnishings. A crucifix hung on one wall; while an uncurtained window looked on to the raging night.

He heard Pedro's footsteps grow fainter in the distance. The wind howled round the eaves and blustered furiously at the window-panes, dashing the rain in a metallic tattoo against the thick glass. Making it secure in its own grease he put the candle on the dressing-table. The shadows crept from their corners and down from the ceiling. The gale howled like a banshee. Slowly and luxuriously Michael drew off his clothes. He stretched his arms above his head in sensuous satisfaction, well content with his magnificently muscled body. Rest—and to-morrow, when the storm had abated, he would go on his way.

He thought of the farmer and his good-looking sister and niece. What a simple natural life they led! Finding the atmosphere a little stuffy he decided to open the window an inch or two. Instantly a blast of chilled air filled the room—extinguishing the candle.

"Blast!" Michael growled. "And I've no more matches."

He groped his way to the bed; knocking his naked shin against the chair as he did so. Drawing the blankets up to his chin, he burrowed his head deep in the feather-filled pillow.

But sleep did not come to him at once. He lay staring into the darkness, listening to the wild cries of the wind. Somewhere a door had blown open and was banging with irregular rhythm. He turned on his side and shut his eyes. The house was silent, but out in the night the wind blustered in impotent assault, and the unlatched door banged against a wall with each angry gust, and the rain streamed down—and at length Michael slept.

It was difficult to explain just why Michael woke two hours later. Certainly the tumult of the storm was as boisterous; and it was equally certain that the cause of his broken sleep was a tiny click. No more indeed, than the lifting of his door-latch. He opened his eyes and peered into the darkness. There was no sound. He told himself that he must have been mistaken, and was preparing to go to sleep again when he heard a board creak, softly but unmistakably. He raised himself on his elbow. Somebody was in his room, somebody who did not wish to be heard. He held his breath. Another cautious step and another gentle creak. Whoever it might be was walking barefooted. Michael decided to let his visitor think that he was asleep. He remembered alarming stories that he had read of lonely houses that had sheltered wayfarers. Well, he hadn't got much of value to tempt a murderer. Someone was standing by his bed. He heard the sound of breathing. He lay tense . . . waiting. Then he shot out his arm and caught that of the intruder, who stood above him. His fingers closed round a frail wrist in a grip of iron.

"Señor," a soft voice whispered, "I had to come. Do not send me away. And be silent, or *he* will hear." There was urgency and fear in the appeal.

Against the square of the window, hardly less dark than the room itself, Michael saw the silhouette of a woman. . . .

Later, when he opened his eyes, he was alone.

At seven in the morning the sky had lightened, although a fine rain still fell with irritating persistency. Michael went to the window and looked out. He washed, and once more dressed himself in his borrowed clothes. He fingered his chin. He supposed that he would have to wait for a shave until he got to Fuiza and the suitcase which he had sent there to await his arrival. He was hungry, and hoped that the family breakfasted at an early hour. When he went down to the living-room he found them already seated round the table.

"Good morning, Señor. We did not wake you—thinking it better for you to sleep," Pedro said. "Maria will give you your breakfast."

Michael bowed a greeting, and glanced at the two women.

"Which one?" he wondered.

Neither gave a sign. Dolores, her head bent over her plate, smiled slightly in answer to his bow. Maria bustled to the stove to bring a hot dish that sizzled in a promising manner. Was it his imagination, Michael wondered, or was his host looking at him intently? He wondered uneasily if he could possibly suspect anything of the previous night's happenings.

"Your clothes are dry, Señor, should you wish to put them on," Maria remarked.

The shirt and breeches, neatly folded, lay on a wooden bench; his riding boots standing stiffly beside them.

"You are too kind." He looked at her directly. "I am more than grateful for all these attentions."

Maria gazed back at him unabashed. "It is nothing, Señor."

"But it is. You have done a great deal for me. You and your daughter," he added.

This time from the corner of his eye he felt certain that Pedro had looked at him sharply. He felt that he had been a fool to say so much. He turned to the man.

"Do you think it will clear?"

The farmer shrugged his shoulders. "One cannot say. Maybe in two . . . three hours. You go to Fuiza?"

"How far is it from here?"

"Thirty miles . . . or a little more."

When, after a substantial breakfast, and having changed once more into his riding breeches, Michael walked along the passage that led from his bedroom to the stairs, he was startled to hear the sound of low sobbing from Maria, who sat by the table at which they had eaten, her head buried in her arms, her shoulders shaking.

"It is terrible . . . terrible." The words were broken by her emotion. Behind her stood Pedro, his face stern.

"What must be . . . must be." He spoke slowly.

Michael started down the stairs, making an unnecessary clatter. Maria raised her head and dabbed at her eyes with the corner of her apron.

"I'm afraid I could not help seeing your distress. Is there anything I could do?"

Pedro answered him. "You? No. You can do nothing, Señor." His words were oddly quiet.

An awkward silence descended on the room. Finally Michael said, "I think it is clearing."

A watery gleam of sunshine struggled to meet the steaming ground.

"If you wish to continue your journey to-day it would be wise to start as soon as you can be ready. I myself have to go as far as Mirano—so I will come with you the first part of your way."

Michael measured him with a glance. It was a wild country through which they were to travel—and they would be likely to meet few people. . . .

"You are too thoughtful. But I could not think of troubling you further."

"It is no trouble at all, Señor. I should appreciate your company."

Michael turned to Maria. "Then I must say good-bye. I cannot thank you sufficiently for your hospitality." Again his penetrating look was met by a pleasant but impassive smile. "I would like to say farewell to your daughter," he ended, somewhat brusquely.

"I am afraid that is impossible," Pedro broke in. "Dolores left here a few minutes ago, and I regret that she will not have returned by the time we go. By your leave I will go and see to your horse. You may help me if you wish."

Together the two men crossed to the stable. "He does not mean to give me an opportunity of talking alone with his sister," Michael thought.

He was sorry that he would not see Dolores again. He remembered her slim beauty, her long-lashed eyes. . . .

For some time Pedro had been silent. The track along which they rode skirted the foothills. The day was clean and fresh after the storm, and the sun had won through to its accustomed brilliance. Michael felt it strike hot on his back and neck, and pulled the knotted handkerchief he wore a little higher for protection against the hot rays.

"In two miles from here we part," Pedro said. "You take the right-hand fork, and I the left." They rode at a leisurely trot; Michael's reins held loosely in his left hand, the other playing idly with his belt. The solitude of their way was very peaceful; only once had they met other men—two peasants driving a battered wagon, drawn by oxen. The scent of washed earth rose sweetly from the countryside. Michael drew great gulps of air into his lungs.

"You have placed me under a great obligation . . ." he hesitated. It was difficult to put into words what he wanted to say. These fellows were so damnably proud. He began again, "Your sister seems worried. After all your kindness to me I wondered if there was anything I could do to be of assistance?"

"Nothing, Señor."

Michael persevered. "I would be only too glad to help. . . . If it is a question of money that is worrying you. . . . If a loan would be timely. . . ."

Pedro drew rein. "I do not ask for charity and will not accept it, in return for what anyone would have done, Señor. My sister's anxiety is of a very different nature. As she told you on your arrival, I am a widower. But I have one daughter, to whom Maria is devoted. And she is the cause of our sadness; for to-morrow she leaves us . . . we fear for ever."

"Dolores . . . is leaving you!"

"No, Señor. Dolores is Maria's daughter. I was speaking of my own. Poor child, she has experienced nothing and will know nothing of life—or love. It is unbearable to think about. And she realises it . . . that is what is so horrible."

His voice was bitter and hopeless.

They rode on. Michael was curious, but felt chary of breaking the silence. They came to the point where the trail forked. A bird began to sing—its clear melody rising joyously to the sky.

"I am sorry for you, my friend," Michael said at last, holding out his hand. "I offer you my full sympathy. Would it be presumptuous to ask what ails your daughter, Señor?"

Pedro looked him full in the eyes, ignoring the proffered farewell.

"She is being taken to-morrow, Señor, because she is a leper."

He wheeled his horse as he spoke and cantered down the left-hand trail. The bird's song of the praise of living swelled in ecstasy.

Michael's knuckles showed ivory white underneath the tightly stretched skin, his nails pressing cruelly into the palms of his hands. His thoughts milled furiously. He remembered Maria and Dolores; their lack of response to his tentative inquiries. He remembered also the sound of a gently closing door as he went to his room. Pedro's words rang in his ears, "She has known nothing of life or love". . . but she had known of the future. . . .

The sun beat on his back; automatically he brushed away a fly that buzzed about his face.

Other birds joined the first in the paean of thanksgiving. A butterfly zigzagged an erratic course among the flowering grasses that bordered the road. The storm was over. Once again the world was good to live in.

Michael rode on, seeing little of the beauty that surrounded him.

THE COCKROACH

Jane sat at the little table and slowly drank her coffee. Peter was late—but then Peter was always late. However hard she tried Jane found it impossible to be angry with Peter, for he would agree with her indignation, saying that she was, as usual, absolutely right; and forthwith dismiss the subject with some absurd and disarming joke.

The Dôme Café was crowded. Jane did not really mind waiting . . . there was so much to see . . . but half an hour! She looked at the people at the next table with a vague annoyance. A party of young Englishmen living in Montparnasse, she surmised, and *dabbling* in art by their care-free appearance. She felt a sharp pang of envy. Here was she, taking her painting very seriously, forced to work like a beaver—and then hardly able to keep herself even with the help of the small monthly cheque that her mother sent her from New York; and there were these jocular, well-fed young men just pleasantly idling away a couple of years in Paris with Art as an excuse for one long whoopee . . . doubtless in magnificent studios where they held ridiculous and certainly drunken parties. Suddenly Jane laughed. She was probably doing her innocent neighbours an injustice, and in any case it was no business of hers. Still smiling, she lit a cigarette.

"Sorry I'm late, darling."

She looked up and saw Peter standing over her. He was wearing a fisherman's jersey of thick blue wool and grey flannel trousers, and his black hair was as tousled as she had known it would be. He sat down and blinked contentedly at the spring sunshine. She thought that she would make some show of displeasure. She regarded him coldly.

"Why *are* you so late?" Jane asked.

"I was fixing up with Adrian about going to the Blue Lizard to-night," he broke off, as a waiter hurried by their table. "Hi! Waiter! Beer . . . and lots of it."

"Bien, Monsieur." The man bustled away.

"The Blue Lizard? Where's that?"

"Somewhere near the Bastille. Very tough . . . grand fun. Real apache stuff!"

"Then I'm coming too!"

"Oh no you're not. You're going to stay peacefully in your flat, and then if I don't return you can barge along with a whole regiment of gendarmes, and stage a terrific rescue scene at the eleventh hour!"

He put his hand on her knee and smiled at her. He loved her serious expression, the grey, rather solemn eyes, the freckled tiptilted nose. She looked absurdly young. He could never believe that she was twenty-three . . . four years junior to himself. And in the autumn, if all went well and he got that job in America from old Crosbie, they would be able to be married and live in a flat . . . in Greenwich Village perhaps. . . .

"But, Peter—don't be a fool—a lot of those dives are *not* safe."

"I know, darling; and that, as you may guess, is half the fun."

The beer arrived in its long thin glass, a symphony of amber and foam.

"Well anyway," she said, "I wish you wouldn't."

"Adrian chucked at the last minute, and that is why Peter went alone. He must have been crazy to do such a thing." Jane was talking quickly. "The police are *no good*, I tell you. They say they've done all they could; and that he was seen leaving the Blue Lizard. But *I* can see that they think Peter had good reasons of his own for disappearing. The French are like that. The man who came here implied that *I* was the good reason. God, how I hate them all! Tony, you must help me. There's nothing else we *can* do."

The young man thus addressed took his pipe from his mouth and uncrossed his long legs.

"But, Jane, if what you think is true, and he has been . . ." he faltered over the word ". . . murdered, it would be madness for you even to think of going to the Blue Lizard. What do you expect to find there?" He raised his hand to stem the protest on her lips. "No, if it will help you, *I'll* go, but *you* can't even consider it."

"Yes I can. Don't you see that it's perfectly safe now? After the police visits and interrogations they wouldn't dare . . ." and

abruptly she began to cry: cruel, tearing sobs that shook her
whole body. "Tony, it's too awful. I know he's dead. I know it. Oh,
God! Peter's dead, I tell you."

"Now, Jane. You can't know it, darling. Don't, honey, don't."
Tony's soft southern voice was comforting.

He held her to him, stroking her hair. After a while she grew
quieter until, spent with emotion, she was wracked by a last piteous shudder.

"Tony—I'll get them . . . whoever did it . . . I'll get them . . . if
it kills me."

"Don't worry, Janey. Don't . . . don't."

The Rue de Bayonne was one of the most sordid and uninviting in the whole of Paris. Ill-lit and badly paved, it consisted of a
depressing expanse of warehouses and squalid shops broken by
an occasional café. Few people disturbed its solitude, and those
who did went about their business with the maximum of des-
patch and self-effacement; oddly furtive. Two policemen stood
talking under a street lamp, legs apart, thumbs tucked into their
belts.

Tony and Jane paused in front of what appeared to be the shut-
tered façade of Maison Levick's storehouse. A battered arch gave
entrance to a narrow courtyard. They peered into the gloom,
uninviting in the extreme.

"It's in here. You're sure you want to go on with it, Jane?"

She squeezed his arm, and Tony knew that as far as she was
concerned there would be no turning back.

"You go first," Jane said.

They went down a flight of stone steps, and pushed open a
heavy door in which was set an iron grille.

The Blue Lizard was like hundreds of cheap café chantants;
the floor coated in sawdust, the low wooden platform for the
performers, the benches and tables stained with the droppings
of innumerable drinks. To-night it was half empty. A dozen burly
men of the navvy class, and maybe half as many women of the
type politely known as "unfortunate," were listening to an old
bawd who, dressed as a ballet dancer in soiled pink tulle, was singing filth to her apathetic audience. Tony led the way to a table

near the door. At their entrance the performer interrupted her song to give them an intent stare.

"We don't seem very popular," Jane murmured, as they received a battery of sullen and uneasy glances from the assembled company.

The proprietor, an old man of revolting aspect, hurried to their table. A purple growth further disfigured his already unprepossessing countenance.

"A beer and a *fine*," Tony said.

While they waited for their order he suggested to Jane that they should ask the man to have a drink with them. "Not," he finished, "that he will say a word that will help us . . . but one never knows."

His prophecy proved correct; the old man not only refused to speak, but he mumbled some obvious excuse and left them immediately after they had been served.

"None of the others look any more hopeful. Lord, I've never seen such a gang of crooks. And that," said Tony, "is that."

"I feel certain that if we keep on we'll discover something," Jane replied. "We must, that's all. And I feel we shall."

"There may be some explanation, darling. After all, it's only four days; and you know how vague Peter is. Probably he went off to Marseilles or somewhere when he was tight, and has written to you and forgotten to post it or something; and even in Paris a body is not exactly easy to dispose of. . . . Peter is not a child, he can take care of himself alright."

"Tony, you're very sweet—but I'm absolutely convinced that something terrible has happened to him." She picked up a dirty card on which the bill of fare was pencilled. "Anyhow, I'm going to stay here for a while, and since we haven't eaten we might as well do so now."

Tony glanced with distaste at their surroundings. "My dear, you can't eat here. You'll most likely be poisoned."

Jane was scanning the menu.

Soup	1.50
Stew	2.50
Bread	.25

"Well, they're not exactly Ritz prices," she said, as she handed him the bill of fare.

Reluctantly he beckoned to the patron and ordered the food. The singer had at last finished her happily limited repertoire, and had sat down at the next table, from which point of vantage she bestowed arch smiles on the unresponsive Tony.

"Jane, I wish you wouldn't insist on staying. This is a lousy place . . . and how can we hope to succeed where the police failed? They're up to all the tricks."

"Because we know he came here, and the police are certain that Peter 'disappeared voluntarily.'"

The ancient houri was now smiling upon Tony with more determined blandishments, ignoring the fact that he already had an "amie."

"Give the old girl a drink," Jane suggested. "She may tell us something."

"If I did we'd have the whole lot over here in half a second. No, the fascinating siren will have to go thirsty a little longer."

A door at the far end of the room was kicked open, and a woman appeared carrying two steaming plates. She was the wife of the man with the tumour, and in appearance and villainy appeared to be an extremely suitable mate for him. From her frouzy grey head to the soles of her ragged slippers, she looked the incarnation of mean squalor. She banged her burden on to the table before Jane and, saying that she would bring the bread, disappeared into her kitchen.

Tony looked at his plate with misgiving. Vegetables and macaroni, mingled with lumps of meat of indefinite origin, floated in a thick congealed gravy of most unappetising appearance. His inspection was interrupted by the reappearance of the maker of this dish carrying in her not overclean hands two rolls, which she placed before them.

"Is there anything else?"

"*Merci*," Tony answered drily. The woman's face glistened with heat from her culinary labours.

"That will be nine francs seventy-five with the drinks." With the back of her hand she wiped the beads of moisture from her forehead.

Tony fumbled in his trousers pocket, and finally produced a tattered five-franc note and various small change. The woman took the money and went away.

Jane picked up her fork and gingerly explored the contents of her plate. "It's not so bad," she said, after a few cautious mouthfuls. And then she found almost immediately afterwards a dead cockroach. It floated in the gravy; its legs, coated with the sticky substance, protesting in mute appeal against its untimely demise.

"Tony, look! Isn't this disgusting? I'm going to show it to that old hag."

And before he could stop her she was across the room and through the door that led to the kitchen. Tony got to his feet to follow her, and then decided to remain where he was. It would be stupid to make a scene in a dump like this. He looked round for the proprietor, but he wasn't visible. He turned his attention to the food. After all, what else could Jane expect if she ate in such places? . . .

Jane found herself in a dirty passage that led to a second door behind which, no doubt, was the kitchen and its unlovely ruler. She walked towards it, anger in her eyes. Pushing the door open she looked in. No one was there. Several saucepans simmered on the stove. She shivered. The door and the table were black with busy cockroaches—vile and big-bodied. She turned round. Hanging behind the door were some old clothes—faded aprons and overalls; boots that had seen better days; a sweat-stiffened leather waistcoat, green with age—a medley of useless rubbish. Then her eyes widened. Rolled up, and crammed under a wooden dresser, she saw a glimpse of some grey stuff, cleaner and in a better condition than the rest of the rubbish. She bent down and pulled. What was it that had been thrust out of sight? The bundle was wedged tightly in the small space between the dresser and the floor, but at last it gave to her efforts.

Jane stood holding a pair of flannel trousers and a fisherman's jersey of thick blue wool.

Peter's! She must go back to Tony and tell him what she had found; and above all she must not panic. She turned towards the door. She must get out before she was discovered. Now she had evidence with which to convince the police. She noticed that the dresser stood between two doors. The loathsome cockroaches were thick in front of the second; hurrying through the crack which was left by shoddy hanging. Perhaps, Jane thought, there was another way out which it would be useful to know—in case there was any trouble. She turned the handle which opened at her touch.

But it was a larder into which the door led, and in it were the remains of what had been a man. As she looked a fat cockroach plopped to the floor, where it lay torpid, in gorged immobility. Only parts of the head, feet and hands of the occupant remained, for the stew was cheap and had been popular; otherwise the bones were left creditably bare by the thrifty cook—and also there were many more cockroaches here than in the room behind her. A novel way of disposing of a body. Tomorrow, doubtless, the menu would be varied. Stew would be "off."

Jane had found Peter.

THE TERROR ON TOBIT

"I suppose you realise," said Daphne, "that in three more days we shall be back in London—for another year?"

"You needn't remind me of that ... the last fortnight has simply flown," Anne replied, shutting her book with a snap. "And I for one have never enjoyed a holiday so much."

The oil-lamp stood, squat and homely, on the plain table in the girls' sitting-room. Outside, the warm August night crept close to the windows, only a slight breeze disturbing the checked curtains. The cottage was one of the dozen modest dwellings that comprised the village of St. Mark's on one of the smaller of the Scilly Islands—relics of that lost land of Lyonesse.

"I hope that you're glad I persuaded you to come?" Daphne, vivid in her dark beauty, smiled at her friend.

"Oh, Daphne, you know I am. It's been absolutely heavenly!"

"Better than Torquay?"

"I've never liked anything better. I can't say more than that, can I?"

There was a knock on the door, and Mrs. Arraway, the mother of the fisherman who owned the cottage, came in for the supper tray. Anne turned to her. "That lobster was delicious. If you only knew how I hated the thought of going back to London."

Mrs. Arraway laughed. She was a pleasant, full-bosomed woman of the islands, where, with the exception of rare visits to Penzance, she had spent her whole life. "I shall be very sorry to lose you, missie. I hope as how you've been comfortable here?"

"It's been perfect," Daphne broke in. "But we've got a favour to ask you."

Mrs. Arraway raised her eyebrows, waiting for her to continue.

"We wondered if Jean would row us over to Tobit to-morrow evening. We want to camp there for the night. It would be such a marvellous ending to our holiday. He could come back for us the next morning. Do you think he would?"

"Well, miss, what do two young ladies like you want to do a thing like that for?" Mrs. Arraway was doubtful.

"Because we want to sleep under the stars—on an uninhabited island. Could anything be more romantic? Oh it would be such fun! Please persuade Jean to take us."

Mrs. Arraway frowned. It was clear that the idea was distasteful to her. But what could one do? Girls were so self-willed nowadays.

"Tobit isn't healthy," she replied after a pause, "that is, not exactly. There's no water on it anyway," she concluded triumphantly.

"That's all right. We can take what we want in a thermos. Please say yes, Mrs. Arraway," Daphne implored.

"Well, I don't know, I'm sure," the landlady answered. "I'll tell you what I will do, miss. I'll send Jean to you and you can see what he says—although I'm certain as how he'll never consider such a mad-cap notion." She picked up the supper tray, and went out of the door, still muttering to herself.

Anne stood by the window looking into the night, with her hands parting the curtains. Against a sky of almost midnight blue, loomed the wild chaos of scarred and riven rocks. The fantastic rocks of the Stilly Isles, that had by day a different and more friendly appearance; calm and less harsh—bearded shaggily with moss and lichen.

"I wonder why these islands have such an atmosphere of enchantment. I've never had the same impression anywhere else. They seem so sad—like gentle faded beauties, dreamily remembering past glories . . . and waiting for the end."

Before Daphne could reply there was a quiet knock at the door.

"I expect that is Jean. Daphne, we *must* persuade him to take us. It would be the most heavenly experience. Come in!"

Jean Arraway strode into the small parlour. He was in the middle twenties, and remarkably handsome, in a strange gipsy way that was unusual among the islanders—but his dark eyes had the faraway dreamy expression that is so often found among those whose mother is the sea.

"Yes, missie?"

"Jean! We want you to help us. Will you?"

"What is it you want me to do, missie?"

"Take us to Tobit to-morrow. We want to stay there for the night. And you can fetch us early on Friday morning. You will, won't you?" Anne smiled at him, exercising her not inconsiderable charm.

"You can't spend the night on Tobit, missie!"

"Why not?" Daphne asked.

"It isn't healthy."

"What do you mean—it isn't healthy? Your mother used the same expression," Anne broke in impatiently.

Jean glanced at her strangely. It was obvious that he was ill at ease; and unwilling to elaborate his statement. There was a short silence in the little room. The girls waited for him to continue.

"It's kind of difficult to explain," he said at last. "But things have happened there. . . ."

"What sort of things?" Daphne was interested.

"Queer things."

"But I thought no one lived there?"

"No one does. But people have gone there once or twice. There was an artist chap the year before last."

"And what happened to him?"

"I don't rightly know."

"Then, why all this mystery?" Anne demanded.

"You see, missie, he never came back. Kind of disappeared."

"But that's impossible. Where could he have disappeared to?"

Jean shrugged his shoulders.

"*No one* rightly knows. There's mighty queer stories about Tobit. It's not meant for us humans."

"What stories?" This was thrilling.

"Well, that artist chap wasn't the only one what went. The year before, there was a lady. A writer I think she was. Insisted on staying there the night—same as you want to do."

"I don't believe it. You're just saying that to put us off. Anyway we're going, if you take us or not—aren't we, Anne?"

"Certainly. A lot of ridiculous superstition."

"I shouldn't if I was you, missie. You wouldn't get none of the islanders to take you. It's real bad. Tobit belongs to the sea, and the sea's creatures."

"Don't be absurd, Jean. Am I to understand that you refuse to take us?"

"I'm sorry, missie."

Fingering his belt, he avoided Anne's eyes.

"Then we'll row ourselves over. And if we aren't back by lunch-time on Friday you'll know the Bogey's got us—and can come over and look for us!" Daphne laughed.

Jean made no reply. He stood there in an awkward silence as if wishing to add some further remonstrance; but realising the uselessness of any such action, contented himself by saying:

"Good night, missies. Maybe in the morning you'll have changed your minds."

Left alone, Anne turned to her friend. "Did you ever hear anything so absurd? It's just because Jean's too lazy to take us—that's all. We'll still go—won't we?"

"Of course we will," Daphne replied. "I wouldn't be put off by a string of lies like that. Although if there was any truth in them, it would be rather . . . curious, wouldn't it?"

The next day, when Daphne and Anne were unlatching the little gate that divided the flower-filled garden of their cottage from the road—little more than a track—that formed the main street of village, they encountered Mrs. Arraway, who, her arms full of vegetables, wished them good morning.

"We didn't have much encouragement from your son last night," said Anne laughingly.

Mrs. Arraway's mouth tightened into a thin line, and an anxious frown wrinkled the placid expanse of her forehead.

"Oh, miss, do give up this mad idea of yours. Jean told me he'd tried to dissuade you. You don't know these islands like we do. Indeed, how could you?"

"But, Mrs. Arraway, what *is* it exactly we have to fear—smugglers or such shady doings?"

"No, miss—smugglers are flesh and blood—but the Thing on Tobit . . . well, no one knows rightly quite what it is, tho' they do say that Tobit belongs to the sea; and that each year the sea demands a sacrifice—in return for all it gives to us."

In spite of the brilliant sunshine and the cheerfulness of the bright island scenery, Daphne felt a chill of foreboding. After all, these islanders might be much nearer to the truth of things than she and Anne.

"The sea missed its sacrifice last year—didn't it? How about that?" Anne teased.

"Don't joke about such a subject, miss—and don't, I beg of you, go to Tobit to-night."

"Nonsense, Mrs. Arraway, we simply must go. We'll be alright . . . don't worry. Would you be very kind, and make us up a picnic basket? We're starting about seven to give ourselves plenty of time to settle down before it's dark"—and the girls swung down the road, two gay figures in their coloured cotton dresses, their towels and bathing suits over their arms.

A group of fishermen was clustered round the few wooden sheds that formed the tiny harbour, overhauling their nets; or sitting silent in companionable groups.

Nothing could have been less sinister or more secure than the tranquil sun-soaked scene. The sea, its calm scarcely broken by a ripple, lay smiling in the sun, flaunting its motley of blues and greens and rich purples—a sea more of the tropics than of our dour northern climate—yet a sea that could on occasion be lashed into a pitiless titan devoid of mercy, a monster of tossing crests and crashing spume-flecked waves that flayed the rocks and crushed the pebbles in grinding torment.

It was after six o'clock when Daphne and Anne, after a long and lazy day on the beach, returned to the cottage. They were full of content, and a pleasurable fatigue, the outcome of hours of amphibian existence; of bathing, and basking, and bathing once more. Their skins were bronzed to a deep tan that made their young prettiness the more effective. Health and well-being wrapped them in their cheerful embrace.

They were met by Jean, his dark hair ruffled, his face sullen. He wore a bleached blue shirt, his sleeves rolled up to his elbows, exposing the tense muscles of his arms; light canvas shoes, and well-worn flannel trousers completed his dress.

"Good evening, Jean."

"Good evening, missie."

The two girls started to walk up the stone flags of the path, Jean following. At the door he spoke.

"You're going to Tobit?"

"Yes."

"Then I'll take you, missie."

"But I thought nothing would persuade an islander to go there?"

Jean flushed. He was intensely uncomfortable. "You see, missie. It isn't right for you to go alone. I'd feel happier myself, like, if you'd let me take you."

"Thank you, we're very grateful." Daphne spoke with sincerity, for she knew the effort that had prompted Jean's offer.

"But you mustn't sleep on the island. That would spoil everything, wouldn't it, Daphne?" then, seeing the man's embarrassment, Anne hurried on, "I mean, you must drop us there, and either come back for us in the morning, or sleep in the boat."

"As you say, missie. And what time will you want to be starting?"

"In about half an hour. We'll meet you at the harbour."

Up in their bedroom, while they were collecting the blankets and rugs necessary for their night's adventure, Daphne said, "You know, Anne, I'm rather pleased Jean will be near us."

"Why, I believe you're scared."

"I'm not at all—but it will mean we can get away if we want to."

"We shan't. Hurry up—we've got to get the food yet—and don't forget the matches."

They found Jean waiting for them in the boat; and in a very few minutes their various packages were stowed away and their journey had begun. Tobit lay about a mile to the west of St. Mark's —a last defiant rock against the barrage of the Atlantic. To their left Daphne saw the island of Samson, uninhabited save for the sea-gulls, although a ruined hut showed where once a shepherd had grazed a few sheep. Tobit itself lay low in the sea—a queer, dark shape, a gigantic beast of a long-forgotten age, stricken and petrified, wallowing in the mill of the waters. Its rocky and forbidding shores riddled with caves gave scant welcome to visitors from the neighbouring islands. On the higher land a coarse sea-grass faintly coloured its spine, dotted with giant and fantastic boulders, monuments of a race lost in the dim ages of the past, perhaps a mountain outpost of Atlantis itself.

Daphne was surprised to find that the boat was nearly there, so lost had she been in her musings. Jean sprang into the sea and waded ashore with the blankets and picnic basket.

From the boat the girls noticed that the rocks had caught a liberal supply of driftwood, so that there would be no likelihood of their fire dying down through lack of fuel.

In a few minutes Jean returned; he had not spoken during the journey, and was evidently liking the expedition no more than in the morning.

"Shall I carry you, missie?"

"No—we'll wade, too," Anne answered.

"Then I'll be helping you to get settled. There's a sandy hollow at the far end of the island that should be sheltered."

They splashed after him to the shore; stumbling over the treacherous rocks slippery with seaweed of a peculiar red colour, and studded with deep pools. Five minutes' walking brought them to a narrow peninsula on the main end of which was a circular patch of sand almost entirely surrounded by great wind-eaten rocks.

"I say, Daphne," her friend said, "looks like a druid's circle, doesn't it?"

"It's one of the fairies' rings," Jean broke in. "There are several such on the islands. The pixies made them."

Daphne laughed. "Yes? I must thank them in that case for our bedroom. By the way, are *you* going to sleep in the boat to-night?"

"It's not right for you to be here by yourselves. It's dangerous, I tell you. Tobit's cursed. It belongs to the sea."

"If you're afraid, why don't you go back to St. Mark's? You can come back for us in the morning." There was a taunt in Anne's question.

"I won't be denying that I *be* afraid. But I won't be leaving you."

"Then you'll sleep—in the boat?"

"No. I'll be on the main part of the island. Near like, in case you're needing me. I'd best stay within hearing."

"Very well." Daphne turned to Anne. "I think we should collect the wood for the fire. Jean and I will get it while you 'unpack.'"

They walked away; and Anne started to make their camp. In her heart of hearts she was none too confident now that night was actually falling . . . and there was no going back. She shivered. Why should her thoughts say that?

There is no going back! She mustn't be hysterical. It might have serious consequences. Still, the feeling remained—a feeling of uneasiness, of dread, almost as if something was menacing them—something unseen watching—and waiting.

Ten o'clock. The firelight flickered eerily, throwing into brief illumination the faces of the two girls, and causing dark shadows to dart momentarily to the very edge of the crackling, salt-saturated fire.

"Don't you think we should try to sleep?" Daphne suggested. "It's after ten."

"Yes. Daphne—I hate to admit it—but I'm frightened. Where's Jean?"

"Over there to the left—about a hundred yards."

"Is he asleep?"

"No, he said he'd . . . watch."

"What for?"

"Goodness only knows. The Bogey, perhaps!" Anne snuggled down more comfortably into her blankets. It was so easy to imagine things, she told herself.

"Good night."

"Good night."

And the waves splashed softly on the shore.

Two hours passed. Daphne stirred restlessly. Then she sat up.

What was that?

The air seemed to vibrate with a high singing sound—oddly penetrating, like the noise of a swarm of giant mosquitoes. It rose and fell in a monotonous cadence. Paralysed with foreboding she lay motionless. She knew she could not bear to listen to it alone for another moment.

"Anne!" her voice was urgent.

Anne did not stir.

"Anne!" she called more loudly.

"Yes. What is it? What's the matter?" She raised herself drowsily on her elbow.

"Don't . . . don't you hear it?"

"Hear what?"

They listened intently. The sea murmured, caressing the rocks with soft, secretive whisperings, glutting the myriad little caves, reluctant to withdraw. But above the whispering of the sea rose that other sound—a high, uncanny whistling, growing more insistent every moment.

"It's the wind in the rocks. Try and go to sleep again."

The fire had burnt down to a heap of glowing embers, and Daphne stretched out her hand to the pile of driftwood. The sticks spluttered and popped as they lay on the hot ashes; but gradually little blue flames crept up into a cone of warmth.

Soon Anne was asleep once more; and Daphne lay on her back gazing wide-eyed at the sky, peppered with a million stars. She was frightened . . . that whistling—what could it be?

"Tobit belongs to the sea—humans have no right there."

Where had she heard those words? Who had spoken them?

She was beginning to feel sleepy. If only that whistling would stop, she might go to sleep. If only it would stop. It seemed that she tossed the victim of insomnia for hours.

Daphne awoke with a start. She was shivering as with an ague. . . . Even now she could not put that terrible dream out of her head.

She had been alone—quite alone by the seashore; and suddenly she had heard a voice cry:

"Two . . . this time it shall be two," and the words had filled her with an indescribable fear, and she had turned to run; but her way had been blocked by a figure, gigantic in stature—and its monstrous shape had moved towards her, and she knew it was the incarnation of evil itself. If it had touched her Daphne was certain that she would have gone mad. . . .

She looked at her watch. Two o'clock. A few more hours and it would be dawn. The fire had died down once more. She stretched out her hand for more wood; but there were only a few sticks left. Anne must have used their supply while she was sleeping.

Without the security of the fire slumber would be impossible. She looked at Anne. Her head lay on her left shoulder, her fair hair falling back from her forehead. Daphne thought she looked very young and very, very sweet. No, she wouldn't disturb her.

The whistling had grown in volume, it seemed to fill the air in a pæan of triumph. She must collect more sticks.... The darkness would be unbearable. She got up and walked out of the circle away from the sandy patch and the friendly embers into the sombre mystery of the island.

The night closed round her.... She was alone, quite alone. But that was ridiculous. After all, Jean was there, and Anne.

She felt afraid: she would walk towards the huge monolith where Jean was watching. She remembered his face, reddened by the light of his fire. His determined expression ... the set look, akin to martyrdom, in his eyes; he knew the danger they were threatened by ... he could only wait.

It was difficult walking. There was no moon; and the tough sea-grass tore at her legs. Where was Jean? There! She caught the glow of the ashes of his fire. She stumbled towards it. But where *was* Jean? She stood on a small hillock peering into the darkness.

"Jean! Jean!" Her voice sounded strangled and strange.

She moved towards the fire; and as she drew nearer she noticed something glistening in the dim light, glistening with a pale phosphorescence. She bent down, the better to discover what it could be. She started back with an exclamation of disgust. The side of the fire where Jean had been sitting was a pool of slime—reeking and foul; the thought came to her that a giant slug might have made that mark—a giant sea-slug. And then real fear gripped her. She was rooted to the spot; stricken with the paralysis of fear. She gazed at the filthy trail at her feet.

"Daphne!" It was Anne's voice—and terror was in it—incredible terror.

"Daphne! . . . Jean! . . . Daphne! Help! Help! Oh, my God!"

The cries suddenly ceased, and a silence, more significant than any clamour, froze her heart.

With an effort she staggered towards their camp, her lips gasping, "I'm coming . . . I'm coming."

She tottered to the top of the rise below which was their sleeping place.

"Anne!" Her scream rose shrilly in the air. "What is it? I'm coming, Anne."

She ran to their camp. Where Anne had lain was a second pool of slime—the same odour of putrefaction . . . and the same trail that led—towards the sea.

Now, if ever courage was needed, she must have it. Such horrors could not be allowed to happen—and she was alone. Anne was gone; and so was Jean. *Something* had taken them. She gazed in horror at the slimy track; remembered the story of the artist who had disappeared. Jean had said, "No one rightly knows what happened to him."

She stumbled on trying to follow the trail of the Thing that had taken Anne. It was difficult to see by the starlight. Occasionally a smear of slime shone on some exposed rock. And always the way led to the sea. Several times she fell, her hands were torn and bleeding, her legs cut by the rocks and the sharp blade-like grass.

"Anne! Anne!"

But the only answer was the faint beating of the waves on the shore. Everything seemed uncannily quiet. Daphne sobbed aloud in her fear.

She realised that the whistling had stopped.

Mrs. Arraway sat in the stern of the boat, her eyes fixed on the island they were approaching. Tobit, in the mellow sun of the late afternoon, presented an appearance of impressive beauty. The jagged outline of her coasts bravely challenged the surrounding waters; the blood-red seaweed gently rose and fell on the waves.

Mrs. Arraway's face was grim, and her eyes were anxious. In the boat were four islanders—sturdy fishermen with muscles of steel, and they rowed in silence. The boat grounded. Mrs. Arraway was the first to reach the shore. She ran to the higher ground.

"Jean! Jean! Miss Daphne! Jean!"

And the caves echoed, "Jean! Jean!" And the sea chuckled as it churned in the channels between the rocks.

Behind her the fishermen padded, heavy-footed, scrambling up the rocks.

"There's one of 'em!" Jim Tregarth shouted.

Mrs. Arraway turned quickly. On the shore below her Daphne sat by a deep pool, her hands full of the red seaweed. She appeared to be unaware of the presence of the fishermen.

Mrs. Arraway ran towards her. She bent down and shook her by the shoulder. Daphne looked up, and there was a great wisdom and understanding in her eyes.

"Jean . . . where's Jean?"

"Jean?" Daphne shook her head. "Jean?"

"And Miss Anne? Tell me, what's happened? Where are they?"

"You'd like to know, wouldn't you? I can see you would. But you won't. . . . You won't. Because nobody knows rightly what happened to them." She laughed to herself. She possessed a great secret, and one that nobody must share. She gave the woman a cunning look; and stroked the seaweed that she held between her fingers. "No," she continued, "nobody will rightly know what happened to them. This time it claimed two. This time. Tobit has taken two!"

For a long time she would not consent to leave the island.

And if you care to go and see her in the square yellow brick building where she was sent, she will beckon you over to her, and drawing your head down to hers will begin to confide her secret to you. But she will never finish it, for she is afraid that if she does the Thing on Tobit will know that she has told—and Tobit belongs to the sea.

THE LAST NIGHT

"Please, doctor," the girl's voice quavered, "please, doctor, let Nurse stay with me. Something awful is going to happen. I know it. Tell Nurse she's to stay with me to-night. It's my last night. I'm going out to-morrow. If you don't tell her to stay I'll kill myself somehow. I swear I will."

The nurse looked at Doctor Patterson with the resigned patient look that adults employ when dealing with a naughty child.

Dr. Patterson smiled. "But, my dear," he said, "what could possibly happen to you? What is it you're afraid of?"

"I can't tell you. I'm afraid to . . . but tell her not to leave me, doctor; tell her she mustn't leave me alone."

He raised his eyebrows at the nurse.

"She won't confide in me. I've no idea what she means, doctor."

"I tell you I daren't. He'd get to hear of it."

"He? Who do you mean?"

"Dr. Morris."

"Dr. Morris?" Patterson was puzzled.

"Yes." Nora almost whispered the answer. She glanced apprehensively round her small white room with its heavily barred windows and narrow spotless bed. There was an air of impersonal and cleanly efficiency that is only found in hospitals and institutions.

"She's a little tired to-night with the excitement," the nurse broke in crisply. "Your mother will be here to-morrow, Nora," she added; "you mustn't over-excite yourself, you know, or we'll have to keep you here a little longer until you are quite well again."

Nora sat down on the edge of her bed. Keep her here longer, would they? For three years she had been in this "mental home" —"A private home," Mrs. Little had impressed upon her friends, "of course Nora is in a *private* home. Poor child. But the doctor says she has been much better lately, and so she'll soon be back with me again."

"Yes, Nora—your mother will come for you tomorrow, and

she mustn't see a tired-eyed child, must she? Now, don't think any more about it, or, as nurse says, you won't be fit to leave. You're not behaving at all reasonably, you know." He believed in humouring the patients . . . to a point! "Just a minute, nurse," he said.

Together they crossed to the door and went outside into the whitewashed corridor. Nora could hear the low murmur of their voices. What were they saying? she asked herself frenziedly. Were they saying that she was mad—that she didn't know what she was talking about? She shuddered, rocking backwards and forwards, her face set masklike with fear. Dr. Morris would come along tonight as he had said he would. She couldn't bear it—she couldn't. His eyes would look at her—those terrible eyes. . . .

Dimly she heard a woman laughing—high, shrieking maniac laughter. It rose shrilly—a penetrating animal scream. The door opened—and the doctor said: "That's number 18 started again. I suppose I'd better see what's the matter." The nurse came into the room. Nora heard the clatter of the doctor's feet on the oil-cloth of the corridor floor.

"Really, Nora, no more of this nonsense, if you please. Come now and get ready for bed. It's eight o'clock."

"Nurse . . . if I tell you, you'll help me, won't you. You'll believe me?"

"That's enough. If you say any more I'll tell the doctor you're bad again. You're a very naughty girl."

Mutely Nora started her evening preparations. If she said any more they wouldn't let her go . . . dear God, that would mean more nights. Perhaps Doctor Morris wouldn't come after all.

"Well, good night, Nora." The nurse switched off the light by the door. "Go to sleep, dear, and don't let me hear another word from you." The door closed with an angry bang.

Nora lay beneath her blankets, her eyes open. Sleep—she must sleep. To-morrow wasn't far away. She was going home to-morrow. She must go to sleep. In the silence she heard the wild laughter of the woman in No. 18. She was bad to-night, the doctor had said. She must go to sleep . . . she must go to sleep . . . she must go to sleep. . . .

Dr. Patterson was worried. He realised of course that it was absurd to pay any attention to Nora's words. She was excited at the prospect of her discharge on the following day, that was all. And yet her terror had seemed so genuine. . . .

He wondered if he should consult Morris; but decided that it would only disturb him needlessly. He mustn't pay any attention. Good Lord, if he took all that his patients said seriously, he would have been one of them years ago. But still—there was something tragic in Nora's pleading. No, he decided, he'd say nothing to Morris. He hadn't seemed very fit lately; he'd been working too hard—and overdoing his pleasures too, if he, Patterson, wasn't mistaken. He was a good-looking brute of a man, and had an extremely strong personality . . . forceful. Dr. Patterson was very precise and liked to amend his thought sentences until they expressed his exact meaning.

Dr. Patterson thought of his own rather meagre form, and sighed perhaps a little enviously. But there was no time for speculation, he told himself; there was too much to do. The woman in No. 18, for instance, would need settling off for the night. A sleeping draught might make the poor soul easier.

Hugh Morris pressed the bell on his desk, and bent his dark head once more over his writing. There was a knock on the door.

"Come in." Hugh's voice was slow and deep. "Oh, Todd," he continued, "I rang to say I shouldn't need you any more to-night. You may go to bed. I've a lot of work to get through, and do not wish to be disturbed under any consideration."

"Very good, sir. And will you be wanting anything left out for you, sir?"

"No, Todd. Good night."

"Good night, sir."

Morris listened to the sound of his retreating footsteps. No—on no account did he wish to be disturbed . . . Todd could swear he had been working in his study all night. He took off his dinner-jacket and shrugged his shoulders into his professional white linen coat. Then he drew soft rubber gloves on to his hands. He crossed to the mirror above the mantelpiece and looked at his reflection with satisfaction.

He saw a man in his middle forties, of immense physique,

with dark hair curling crisply back from his forehead, strong chin, and a firm mouth with thick rather negroid lips. It was a good-looking face—but not in any way remarkable, with the exception of the eyes. Large and of a deep blue, they burned with the light of fanaticism. His enemies said that his eyes were those of a demented man. His lady friends, and they were many, said that they were "terrified by Hugh's eyes—they're hypnotic." But Morris really paid little attention to what friends or enemies said —he had only one aim and object in his life, his profession—the study of the human brain—and to-night . . . to-night, he smiled exultantly, he was going to test his theory of how far a subject under hypnotic influence could resist bodily pain. He glanced at the time. It would be safer to wait an hour.

The moonlight flooded Nora's tiny room, bleaching it of what little colour it possessed. For hours it had seemed to Nora that she had lain awake, stark with fear, listening, listening for those sure and heavy footsteps that she knew so well. She would have run out into the corridor, but the door was self-locking, and could only be opened from the outside, unless one had a key, and she would get into trouble if she were found wandering in the corridors.

And then, when her taut nerves told her she could bear the suspense no more, sleep had come to her.

The clock over the gateway of the Menyham Mental Home struck two. The building was in darkness, except where one patch of dull orange showed the room in which the nurse on night duty sat reading or knitting. It was seldom that she was disturbed by her patients.

Softly Morris opened the door of his dispensary. The passage was deserted. Like most men of great physical strength he could, when occasion demanded it, move as lightly as a cat. Outside room 18 he paused. There was no sound.

He noted with satisfaction that the patient had responded to the sleeping draught that Patterson had prescribed. His hand caressed a small scalpel in the pocket of his coat—lovingly fingering the cold metal.

*

Nora opened her eyes. Surely, oh surely, it was nearly morning. She glanced anxiously at the window. It was so difficult to judge time. In a few hours her mother would be here. It was to-day she was leaving. Her mother! Oh, it would be good to be home again; among colour and warmth and friendly interest.

A slight noise outside the door startled her. She saw a thin wedge of light. It slowly widened. Fascinated, she could not tear her eyes away. Doctor Morris! She knew that there had been no chance of escape. Why hadn't she told nurse—insisted on Dr. Patterson listening to her. He'd told her only that morning. "It's to be our secret, my dear," Dr. Morris had said, "you understand that, don't you? If you tell anyone that I shall come, I'll kill you."

She shivered as she thought of his blue eyes blazing down into hers. She had seemed paralysed, incapable of speech. And now he was here. . . .

Hugh's broad bulk filled the lighted space.

"Doctor Morris," Nora whispered the words.

"Be quiet, you little fool."

He stepped inside the room and leant against the door. The gentle click of its closing was very clear in the silence of the room. With two strides he was standing over her. Her face, a pallid moon-blanched oval, looked pitifully up at him. "Doctor Morris," she repeated.

Hugh sat on her bed, which creaked protestingly beneath his weight. His hands caught hers.

"Nora—look at me." His face was very near her—his large square teeth gleaming startlingly white against the tan of his skin.

"Nora . . . remember what I said to you this morning. You told no one I was coming here—did you?"

"No one, doctor."

"Look at me," his grip on her hands tightened. "You will do as I say—do you hear?" he spoke without expression. "You feel no pain—there is no such thing as pain. Repeat that after me. There is no such thing as pain. There is no need to be frightened. Repeat it. . . . There is no need to be frightened. . . . 'There is no such thing as pain.' "

"There is no such thing as pain."

"Pain exists only in the imagination."

"Pain exists only in the imagination."

Gradually Nora felt her consciousness slipping. She was tired —oh, so tired. She couldn't keep awake any longer. . . . Something in the back of her mind told her it was dangerous to let herself go to sleep, very dangerous. But really she didn't care dreadfully any more. She wished Doctor Morris would stop looking at her. His terrible eyes seemed boring into her head . . . she tried to cry out —and then everything went black.

Hugh saw her expression go blank. With a soft grunt of pleasure he released her hands. Still peering steadfastly into her face he pulled out the small gleaming scalpel. He touched her hand with the cold steel, but the girl gave no sign of feeling it.

"Nora—can you hear me?"

There was no response. Carefully he picked up the tiny instrument. The blade glimmered in the cold light of the moon. He made a small incision on the back of the girl's hand. Immediately a thin scarlet line showed on the white flesh.

"Pain exists only in the imagination." Hugh was triumphant. His experiment had started well.

Nora was moving her hand, vaguely and without purpose. She was smiling—a silly meaningless smile. He watched what would happen. Abruptly her hand quivered and crawled spider-like across the sheet towards his. It grasped the scalpel. Morris stood up. It was interesting, he thought, to see what her next move would be. His scientist's fascination rooted him to the spot.

"Nora—make a small cut on your left thumb—do you hear me? There is no such thing as pain."

The girl hesitated. Morris was tense with excitement—if the subject inflicted injury on herself without suffering. . . .

Nora was standing facing the window, her face clear in the moonlight; calmly she raised her right hand holding the knife. For a moment she stood quite still, then, with a deliberate movement, she moved her hand across her throat.

"Stop." Hugh's voice was frenzied.

It seemed to his horrified gaze that the girl had two mouths —two red smiling mouths. And the lower one was in her throat.

With a little sigh she sank to the floor, and he saw the blood gushing over her thin regulation nightgown.

"Nora——" he stood spellbound, petrified. It seemed to him that there was blood everywhere—on the floor, the bed, on his hands. His one thought now was to get away. No one had seen him leave his dispensary; if he could get back to his study with the scalpel, perhaps, when the tragedy was discovered, he could "find" an ordinary table knife—the explanation would be that Nora had hidden it herself, had planned suicide.

He turned to the door, and only at that moment did he realise the terror of the situation. The key was on the outside—he himself had closed the door, and he was a prisoner until the morning. He glanced at the bloody heap on the floor. He must keep his head, he told himself. He took a step towards the window, and his foot slithered. Blood—blood everywhere. He crept to the window, but the iron bars mocked him. Desperately he tore at them with the terrific force of his giant muscles. He must keep calm . . . he mustn't lose his nerve. It depended on himself alone. He stumbled back to the bed and sat there, his head in his hands, staring unseeingly before him.

Outside the clock struck three. Three o'clock! He must hurry, the night nurse went her rounds at half-past three.

The figure on the floor moved . . . he could swear that he saw it move.

"Keep your head . . . keep your head. She didn't suffer—no, of course not, because there is no pain."

He wondered who that was he could hear talking. Of course, it was his own voice. You can't be frightened of your own voice. "It's only in your imagination. There is no pain. There is no pain—oh, let me out! God help me, let me out!" He was screaming, screaming with the full force of his lungs. "There is no pain, I tell you—it only exists in the imagination. I've proved it. Proved it. Proved it. Let me out!"

He flung himself against the door, battering upon it until his hands bled, his great strength impotent. He could hear voices in the corridor, frightened whisperings. Then a man's urgent tones. That must be Patterson, Hugh thought. Then more voices—the warders.

"Let me out—I've proved it. I was right ... right. Pain is an illusion!"

Cautiously the key was turned. Framed in the door was a group of men, behind them the frightened faces of the nurses.

"Morris!" Patterson was wide-eyed with horror.

"I've proved it, Patterson—there is no pain." Hugh was laughing wildly, triumphantly. "Do you realise what it means? I've won. I've conquered pain."

AN EYE FOR AN EYE

The dining-room was lit by the shaded glow of four candles set in old glass candlesticks, leaving the corners of the room indistinct with wavering shadows.

Jimmy Clinton looked at his guests. On his right sat Miss Geraldine Victor. She was a distinguished looking woman dressed in deep wine-coloured velvet, that set off the raven beauty of her hair, parted severely in the middle, and drawn into a knot on her neck. She had reached the middle thirties, and was one of the most successful of the "precious" novelists.

Next to her was Jimmy's wife, Naomi. Fair and tiny, she made a perfect foil to the other's dark beauty. She leaned forward in her chair, the fingers of her left hand drumming on the highly-polished surface of the table.

"But, Jimmy—if the police *know* who's done it, why can't they arrest the man?"

"Because, darling, the evidence is inconclusive."

"You see, Mrs. Clinton," Sir Henry Mathews broke in, "a man can only be tried once for any murder, and the police are reasonably certain that sooner or later he will give himself away."

"Or that the missing link in the chain will be filled in," Jimmy concluded.

"Exactly." Sir Henry poured himself a second glass of port.

"Anyway, I'm sure the chauffeur did it, and I think it is scandalous that he should get off scot free," Naomi repeated obstinately.

"Of course he did it. I wish I had the power of deciding the sentence," Geraldine added with malice.

Sir Henry smiled at Jimmy. "And they say that women are the gentler sex. . . ."

"But it was a ghastly crime. That poor girl. I was told that the details were too horrible to be printed. She was only sixteen, you know. Such men should be killed in some frightful way. Hanging is too good for them," Geraldine insisted.

"As it happens I've known Dr. Peters for many years," Sir

Henry's quiet words were all the more arresting in contrast to Geraldine's vehemence.

"Did you know him well? And the girl? Oh, how thrilling!" Naomi was flushed with excitement.

"I knew Angela, yes. No, I shouldn't say very well. She was one of the loveliest little things I ever saw. I could hardly believe when I saw in the paper the dreadful thing that had happened. But when you get to my age, my dear young lady, you will be surprised at nothing."

"And don't you think the chauffeur—Yarrow, wasn't that his name?—did it?"

"Undoubtedly," Mathews replied. "But if the proof isn't conclusive, there's nothing you can do, my boy."

"I think it's criminal to let him go free. He'll only do it again. Those people always do," Naomi said. "Somebody ought to put him away and no questions asked."

"You may be certain that the next time they will get him."

"I should hope so—but by then one more human life will have been sacrificed needlessly."

"Well, Naomi, what do you suggest I should do?"

"I don't suggest that *you* should do anything, but somebody should. The girl's father, or brother or somebody."

"Angela was an only child."

"I say, Sir Henry, this fellow Peters isn't *the* Doctor Peters, is he?" asked Jimmy.

"He is."

"Not the man who has done such wonders with the thyroid experiments? Then why," questioned Geraldine dramatically, "does he choose to live in Wimbledon?"

Sir Henry laughed. "Because," he said, "when one gets older one appreciates a little rest and quiet, Miss Victor."

"Yet it's rather strange when one considers that if he hadn't lived so near the Common his daughter might be alive to-day."

"As to that, there are many lonelier places within half the distance of Hyde Park Corner."

"Don't let's talk any more about murders," Naomi shuddered. "If you're ready, Geraldine, we'll leave them to gloat over the ghastly details."

Jimmy rose to open the door for them. In the doorway Naomi turned back to fling a parting admonition, "And don't be too long, Jimmy, with your ghoulish chatter—or we'll be late for the play."

Left alone the two men sat silent for a moment, each thinking of the horrible tragedy that had held the public interest for the last few days.

"Brandy?"

"No, thanks—a little more of this excellent port if I may."

Jimmy poured himself a stiff brandy, and then turned to his guest.

"And what do you think will happen to this man Yarrow, now? It'll be damned difficult for him to get a job, won't it?"

"Extremely. He'll most probably try for a new start in the colonies."

"Or change his name?"

"It may not be necessary. If he really has done it, he won't get off. Few murderers do, you know, when they have once been suspected. He'll make a slip sometime."

"It was a filthy business."

"More filthy than you know, Jimmy. As Miss Victor said, the details were too disgusting for the public to know. And she was only sixteen. . . ."

"Jimmy!" Naomi could be heard calling in the hall.

"All right. Coming, darling!" Clinton called back. "Frightfully sorry to hurry you like this," he continued to Sir Henry, "but I think Naomi's anxious to see the curtain go up."

George Yarrow sat on the edge of the bed in the little room he rented at No. 77, Elderton Road, Wimbledon. It was small and dreary, but the rent he paid was only eight shillings a week, and his landlady kept it tolerably clean. His brain still felt stunned after the ordeal he had just been through. The court had been hostile; and it was obvious that everyone had thought that he was guilty. And he was—it had been that fact that had given him such desperate courage. And his defence had been so weak. He had been for a walk in Hyde Park he had maintained—and yet they couldn't disprove it. And an accused man was innocent until proved guilty in an English court. He had good reason to be glad of that. But at one moment things had looked pretty black. In the thirty years of his life Yarrow had never endured such hidden fear as he had felt as, one by one, damning items of evidence against him had been piled up.

It had been that atmosphere of antagonism and unrelenting hostility that had put the wind up him, that and the pitiless eyes that had searched his face, and the jeers of the crowd who had waited to see him leave the building.

Two hysterical girls had called out "Bravo, George!"—he hadn't known them. He wondered who they were—they had liked his looks perhaps. He smiled as he looked at his wide shoulders and athlete's chest. He'd never lack for girls, that was quite certain.

But he was still worried. He frowned as he remembered the hoots of the crowd.

"Murderer."

"Dirty Swine."

"Lynch the ——"

He had been hurried into the waiting motor car.

There was one thing that surprised him. Old Peters taking him back. He wasn't so sure that he wanted to go; he thought the best thing was to get right away, Canada or Australia—but again, that might look suspicious. No—he'd made up his mind to stay with the old man for a time at any rate. It would certainly be hard to get a job under his own name, and if he changed it some blasted busybody would be sure to make it his business to bring it to the notice "of whom it might concern."

He took off his shoes and swung his legs on to the bed and lay down, his hand fumbling for a packet of cigarettes. He lit one. He must think all this out—see what fresh danger, if any, must be thought of. God—but it had been a close thing. The gallows had seemed uncomfortably near. He looked at the window with narrowed eyes, through the cloud of cigarette smoke, his mind probing ceaselessly the events of that fatal evening.

All through the questioning he had stood with his big red hands clenched, saying as little as possible, repeating his statement that he could throw no light on the case, that he had taken a walk in Hyde Park as it was his evening off, and that it wasn't his fault if no one had seen him. He broke out into a sweat as he remembered how he had searched the crowded court room for Nelly's face. But she hadn't been there. He found that difficult to understand. Still, she was a good sort, Nelly, and had loved him once.

After "it" had happened, his brain had cleared, and his one thought had been to get away. He had made for the nearest road on which the 'buses ran. As he was waiting in a small knot of people, he had seen Nelly coming. Hastily he had looked away. Nelly's step quickened as she had seen George. It had been some weeks since they had met, and she wanted to talk to him—dreadfully. She went up to him, and put her hand on his sleeve. She thought how handsome he looked. He appeared startled to see her—anxious to get away.

"George, I must speak to you."

"Well, what is it?" He was sullen, and there was panic in his heart.

"Why are you so cruel to me?" She pronounced it "crool." "Is it because you've got another girl? Because if that's it, I've got the right to you, George." Her eyes sharpened with suspicion.

And then he had seen a 'bus coming; he didn't care where it was going, brutally he shook her hand off his arm and jumped on to the platform.

Nelly had stood looking after him, as the 'bus gathered speed. No—he shouldn't get away from her like that. She'd show him. She ran a few steps into the road—heedless of the warning cry of a woman behind her. Then something hit her with the force of a battering ram—and she knew no more.

Having gained the 'bus George gave no backward glance. Hell! Just his luck to have met Nelly at that time when he might want to prove he had been far away. He guessed he'd have to square her if any suspicion fell on him. Take her out of nights. He smiled as he anticipated her ready acceptance; she wasn't a bad little thing really, with her big dark eyes and soft fluffy hair. And he reckoned now that she had done the square thing by him, saying nothing when all the newspapers had been publishing his description.

Yarrow crushed out his cigarette. Yes—he'd have to see her and fix things—he thought he knew how.

Old Peters had told him to report the following morning, but he thought it would look better if he went this evening. To show he was keen and appreciative like. Appreciative! If the old codger only knew. And he must change into his uniform.

He rolled off the bed and unbuttoned his coat. Five minutes later, back in the dark blue coat and breeches of his service, he was bending down and fastening the shiny black gaiters round his thick legs—muscular as a footballer's. He picked up his cap. Whew! It had been a near thing. He straightened his tie and with a final glance in the mirror swaggered out of the room.

Dr. Peters sat in a deep armchair in front of the blazing fire in his study. He looked tired, and there was pathos in the stoop of his shoulders. The events of the last few weeks had aged him. Angela had been his only child. Even now he could scarcely realise that this horror had happened to him. Yarrow was guilty, of that he had no doubt. Therefore, he reasoned, it was best to have him under observation, where he could keep an eye on him. If only somebody could be found who had seen him near the scene of the crime, but reliable witnesses are wary of swearing away another's life. His eyes dilated as he gazed into the glowing core of the fire.

Yarrow's life! He would crush it out with as little compunction as he would that of a poisonous insect. He had tried hard in the court to keep the hatred out of his face when he saw the brutal hulk of his chauffeur in front of him. Sometime, from someone, that missing link of evidence must come. Until that time he could only wait—and while waiting observe . . . and ponder.

He got up and pressed a bell by the fireplace. A few moments later Smith, his butler for many years, entered.

"You rang, sir?"

"Yes. Bring me a whisky and soda, will you? And, Smith! Yarrow is returning to my service to-morrow."

"Yarrow, sir? But . . ."

"The verdict was murder against a person or persons unknown, Smith. In that case Yarrow is innocent. That is all."

"Very good, sir."

The butler's face was impassive as he made his way back to the servants' quarters. Whatever his own thoughts may have been, the lower servants would respect their master's wishes. He would see to that.

Dr. Peters smiled a little grimly into the fire. Here he was, perhaps the most miserable and pain-wracked of men, and yet he was envied by thousands of his fellow-beings. He was "a successful man"; he had reached the topmost peak of his profession. He knew perhaps more about the secrets of the human body— the intricate workings of the brain, and the functioning of the glands, than any other man living. His word was law to his admiring colleagues, his opinions were unquestioned, and he had had the opportunity of turning down a baronetage. For why should he want one? He had no son—only Angela. A flicker of pain crossed his face. He must not think of Angela.

Nelly Torr opened her eyes. Where was she? Her head ached and she was unable to turn on her pillow to see where the sound of muffled voices came from, or who it was that was talking. She saw in front of her a strip of wall, white-washed, and without ornamentation, and she was lying in a narrow white bed. And then another blinding flash of pain seemed to cleave her head in two, and once more she relapsed into unconsciousness.

It was dark when next she woke up, and there was silence in the room. Again she tried to turn her head, and again something impeded her. Then she heard a faint rustle by her bedside, and a nurse in a stiffly starched cap spoke to her.

"Yes, my dear? And how are you feeling now?"

"My head. It hurts something terrible! What happened? Where am I?"

"Now don't you worry, and don't ask questions. Drink this and then have another nice sleep." She held a glass containing some pinkish fluid to Nelly's lips.

Nelly suddenly found that she was very thirsty, and drank it gratefully. The last thing she remembered was the nurse's efficient hand gently smoothing her pillow and arranging the sheets.

She awoke the next morning feeling considerably refreshed in spirit, but extremely sore in body. She learnt that she had been knocked down by a motor car and had been brought to the hospital, where she had lain unconscious for two days. If she kept quiet and did what she was told, the nurse added, there was no reason why, in a week or two, she shouldn't be as right as rain.

"But it was a very nasty knock, dear, and more haste less speed, you know."

She smiled brightly and hurried from the room to a case in the next ward.

Nelly occupied a private room, since she needed perfect rest and quiet. She found it very peaceful, and lay looking in front of her and thinking of what had happened. She remembered her meeting with George, his coldness to her and her jealousy. Well, she'd just show him—the big rotter.

"Like a look at a paper, dear?" the nurse asked kindly one morning a few days later.

"I don't think so, thank you. What's the news?"

"Nothing very much. There's a new Chevalier film coming on this week, some trouble in Bulgaria or some outlandish place— oh, and a horrible murder at Wimbledon."

"Wimbledon?—that's where I come from. Who was it?" A guilty thrill of the possibility of knowing the murderer or the victim stirred in Nelly.

"Some girl. The body was terribly injured, so it says."

"Have they got the chap what did it?"

"Not yet. But they suspect a chauffeur, I think it was. Or a footman. Anyhow it was somebody in service."

"Wonder if I know him. I've several boys in service. It's awful what they do do nowadays, isn't it? Why, I'll never feel safe again." She giggled inanely.

"I've some more news for you," the nurse went on. "The doctor says you can get up for a little while this afternoon—and if you continue to improve at this rate you'll be leaving us next week, probably on Monday." She fussed around the room, lowering the blind, and moving the glasses on the bedside table. "And your landlady sent some more of your things this morning," she concluded.

In a way Nelly was sorry to be leaving the Hospital. She had been very comfortable there, and the return to her work in the stuffy tea-shop was, at that moment, extremely uninviting.

Her thoughts returned to George. She'd get even with him somehow—see if she didn't.

On the Sunday afternoon, the day previous to her departure, Nelly sat on her bed gossiping to the nurse, who had brought in a copy of a Sunday paper of a popular nature, that enjoyed a circulation of several millions. One of its features was a weekly competition for those who deemed themselves judges of dress, and there are very few women who do not see themselves in that guise. Also she carried a copy of the last week's number, to show Nelly the choice she had made. Together they inspected the occasionally fantastic garments, arranging them in their order of merit. At length, a decision having at last been reached, nurse bustled off in search of pen and ink to fill in the fateful form.

Left by herself Nelly idly turned the pages of the week-old journal. From the printed page her eyes were held by the poorly printed photograph of a handsome smiling face. Underneath she read:

"GEORGE YARROW, THE MAN THE POLICE QUESTIONED."

Laboriously but intently she read of the man's explanation of his being in Hyde Park at the time of the crime, and of his flat denial that he was anywhere near the Common.

Nelly held the paper in her hand and stared at the report. She thought of his hurry to leave her . . . and of his jilting her. Should she go to the police? She wanted time to think.

The next day Nelly left the Hospital, but her mind was restless. What had she better do? The police? No—there was no knowing where going to the police would get you, in her opinion, and it didn't do a girl any good getting mixed up with the law. Who then could she tell? . . . Dr. Peters?

It was half-past ten as she hurried that evening towards Dr. Peters' house. It was quite a long walk, and Nelly's resolution was weakening as she threaded her way through the crowded and brightly lighted streets. Suppose George should meet her going in . . . find out that she had told on him! She was approaching the garish entrance to the "Splendide" Cinema, and people were drifting out from the show. *Throbbing Hearts*, the posters proclaimed, was being featured that week.

There were mostly couples coming out, she noticed, with a pang. One of them had halted in the entrance. The girl was smiling up into the face of her companion. She was highly made-up, and not at all "classy," Nelly considered. She seemed to be arguing with the tall young man. Suddenly he turned and stood facing towards Nelly, but with his face bent to his companion, as if urging her. His hands were thrust deep into his trousers pockets.

It was George. Nelly paused and pretended to look into a shop window, slyly watching him from the corner of her eye. His soft hat was tipped rakishly at an angle, his purple tie boasted a flashy tie-pin that she had given him, a thick gold albert stretched across his broad chest between the upper pockets of his waistcoat. His shoes, extravagantly pointed, were of gleaming yellow leather. Nelly recognised that he was dressed to impress.

"Oh, I couldn't *reely*," the blonde was protesting coyly, "whatever would people say? Oh, you are a one!"

They turned away, her arm tucked through that of her companion; still half-heartedly expostulating.

If anything had been needed to strengthen Nelly in her purpose she now had it. She walked quickly on her errand. She'd show him! She'd show him—and that fancy piece of his!

She reached the entrance to the drive of Dr. Peters' house, and started up the tree-darkened gravel.

Dr. Peters sucked at his pipe. He turned to Nelly.

"And you are quite certain, Miss Torr, that it was Yarrow you saw. You could not have been mistaken?"

"Mistaken, I should say not." She laughed shrilly. "If anybody ought to know George Yarrow, I should. I knew him most intimate . . . at one time."

"And you would be prepared to sign a sworn statement to this effect?"

"If you say so, Dr. Peters, of course. But I don't want no trouble with the police, mind."

"You won't have any, I can promise you that. For the present you must tell nobody. The matter is perfectly safe in my hands. I have your word for it?"

"Righto, Dr. Peters. Well, I'll be going now. And remember you've promised that George shan't know as how I've let on."

"I have already given you my word, Miss Torr." He rang for Smith to show her out. The butler conducted the visitor to the door with a haughty and condescending air.

When he had closed the door he returned to the study. "Is there anything I can get you, sir?"

"No, Smith. I want to talk to you. How long is it you have been with me. Fifteen years?"

"Sixteen, sir."

"And you were fond of Miss Angela, were you not?"

"You know how I felt, sir. If she'd been my own daughter . . ."

"Very well. Now listen to me."

For half an hour the two men talked earnestly. At the conclusion of the interview Peters stood up. Solemnly they shook hands.

"And, Smith . . . ring up Mr. Carter and say that I would be pleased if he would dine with me to-morrow. Say that it is very important. That is all. Good night."

"Good night, sir."

Peters sat for a long time in his study, the fire light gleaming on his white shirt-front. Yes—Tony Carter must be in on this. Tony, who had been the heavyweight champion at Cambridge last year. He and Tony and Smith should manage it between them. An eye for an eye . . .

Smith knocked on the surgery door. Behind him stood Yarrow carrying a small bag of tools.

"What is it?" the doctor's voice called.

"Yarrow is here, sir, to see to the lights."

"All right. One minute."

Yarrow was annoyed. He considered that eleven o'clock at night was an extremely inconvenient and inconsiderate hour to be called out. He had had a "date," which he had been forced to break, and had had no opportunity of putting off the lady. Also he had just changed from his livery and had had to put it on again, knowing how fussy the old bastard was!

The door opened, and the butler stood aside to let him enter. Yarrow looked around him with interest—he had never visited the surgery before.

Dr. Peters was dressed in his white "working" clothes. Yarrow stood before him, his cap in one hand, the bag in the other. The door shut behind him.

"Put up your hands."

A man's voice barked the order. Instinctively Yarrow wheeled round, and found himself looking down the barrel of a revolver, behind which was the steady gaze of Tony Carter.

"What's the meaning of this? What's the game?" Yarrow spoke gruffly.

"That we know you for a murderer," Peters said quietly. "Some days ago the missing piece of evidence came into my hands. If I felt so inclined I could hand you over to the police—to hang by the neck until you were dead. But hanging is too good for swine like you. The sworn statement that you were seen near the scene of the crime by one who knew you well, is in my possession."

Smith stepped forward and snapped a pair of steel handcuffs on Yarrow's wrists.

"What are you going to do to me?" He was frightened now, deadly frightened. The set faces of the three men were merciless. Peters came towards him, a pad in his hand. Yarrow smelt a sweet sickly odour. He started to kick, but was thrown to the floor by Carter . . . he was stifling . . . choking . . . he could hear low grunts and curses as a chance kick got home, but the sounds seemed very faint, a long way off.

When he came to himself Yarrow found that he was lying on a long white table. He tried to move his arm, but something held it in a vice. His legs were confined in a similar manner by thick leather straps. He lay there, stark naked and powerless underneath a brilliant glare from the light that hung above the operating table. As far as he could see, he was alone. He felt sick, his body wracked with nausea. He strained at the straps, the muscles of his arms standing out in knots. He turned his head and saw on his right his clothes huddled in a heap on the floor. His coat and waistcoat, the breeches, the thick boots and leggings, and the peaked cap of his uniform.

He mustn't be frightened, he told himself; old Peters was trying to bluff him, that was all. He thought he'd panic him into confessing his guilt—well, he'd show the old bastard who was the better bluffer of the two. He didn't believe the old —— had a statement at all. He'd have the law on him for this, see if he didn't.

The straps were chafing his arms, and angrily irritating the skin round his ankles. He wondered where the old man was, and what fresh devilry he was planning. He wished he'd come back, this waiting was getting on his nerves. He pulled at the straps, but only hurt himself the more. His face grew red, and sweat broke out on his forehead and hairy chest; his breathing became uneven with the physical efforts of his struggles.

He heard a door open, and soft footsteps crossed to where he lay. Dr. Peters still wore his white coat, and he was wheeling a table on which lay gleaming rows of knives and forceps and queer, contoured probes.

"You bloody —— you can't do this to me. I'll have the police on you." Yarrow was terrified.

"I do not think you will, my friend. I am not going to kill you —and if you go to the police they will assuredly hang you."

"But I tell you I didn't do it. I swear I didn't."

Peters paid no attention. Again Yarrow felt the sickening pad pressed on to his mouth.

During the hours that followed Yarrow suffered hell. Never entirely conscious, yet never unconscious, his body endured blinding, rending pain. At intervals he fainted, only to recover to endure more agony. He lost all sense of time, the world had become for him a place of unbelievable torture, his nerves cried out for respite, his brain shrieked that he could stand no more. From time to time there were periods of near oblivion, periods of bliss it seemed to Yarrow—but these were succeeded by more spasms of pain each surmounting in intensity the previous ordeal. Wave after wave of blinding agony.

Dr. Peters worked as one possessed. All his vast knowledge of the human body was called to play a part. No one was permitted to come near the laboratory save Smith. The servants were told that he was engaged in vital experiments and must on no account be disturbed.

During the months that followed Dr. Peters spent many hours in his surgery. Separated from the main body of the house, with which it was only connected by a covered corridor, the doctor had complete privacy. After a time, even the butler was forbidden to enter the room itself, although he frequently brought his employer's meals on a tray to the door, where he left them.

It was June when Yarrow had disappeared; and now January held London in its frigid grip.

One day Smith came down the passage to collect the luncheon tray. The door was open a few inches, and the sound of the cracking of a whip echoed between the bare walls. He could see Peters standing over a figure that crouched on the floor chained to a staple driven into the wall. The creature snarled and twisted to avoid the cruel leather thong that slashed mercilessly at its unprotected body. Smith could hardly believe his eyes. What could this travesty be, this monster that grovelled at Dr. Peters' feet? Its hands were bound together—its legs bent and calloused. The arms, in contrast to the fore-shortened thighs, hung ape-like with simian looseness from the wasted body, whose giant bones were starting through the skin. The face was the face of an old man, wrinkled with age and fear, but with a sly cunning lurking behind the rheumy eyes. A thing of horror—of pity.

Yarrow's disappearance was accepted as a guilty man's flight, for none of his fellow-servants believed him innocent; in fact, "below stairs" they had none of them doubted that he would make his getaway at the earliest opportunity.

Jimmy and Naomi Clinton sat impatiently in their motor car —a long low Invicta—they were late for lunch; and the block of traffic in the Tottenham Court Road was very exasperating. Naomi gazed idly at the passers-by.

"Jimmy, look! What a disgusting sight—what do you think it is?"

"From the show at Olympia, perhaps." He looked at the grotesque figure ambling along the pavement. The jostling lunch-hour crowds giving it as wide a berth as the pavement permitted.

"Isn't it pathetic? Why are things like that allowed to live?"

"The Lord knows!" He was irritated by the delay. "We're going to be awfully late, darling." The traffic block broke and the Invicta slid forward. Naomi turned to look after the bizarre ape-like figure, alone in the crowd, an outcast for ever from its fellow creatures. She thought how terrible it was that it would never know human relationships—at the best, only pity and commiseration—or laughter and curiosity.

Naomi was puzzled by the decrees of a blind fate. Why were such abortions permitted to exist—to live? Inconsequently she remembered the terrible murder at Wimbledon, and wondered if the man had ever been caught. She turned to Jimmy.

"Darling, did they ever find the Wimbledon murderer?"

"He got off scot free." His eyes were fixed on the traffic ahead of him. "Lord knows what happened to him. Probably found it difficult to get a job—but apart from that slight inconvenience —yes."

The car drew up in front of the Ritz Hotel.

"Come on, darling—we're very late; so don't be too long doing your face."

Their life went on . . . and Yarrow, shambling down the Tottenham Court Road, suffered—from "a slight inconvenience."

HENRI LARNE

Nina and John had been married nearly two years when they decided to go abroad for their holiday. They lived in a small flat in St. John's Wood, a place of light and air and new chintz, and cream-painted walls. The flat was really the top floor of an old-fashioned house hastily converted to the needs of the impoverished post-war young who wished to cut domestic responsibilities to a minimum. And so we find No. 16, Jeremy Road, housing eight people, living five separate lives under the one slate roof.

The ground floor was occupied by the Treymaines, a quiet couple who were something of a mystery to their fellow tenants. Above, two young men had bed-sitting rooms with a communal bath. The third floor housed the Misses Togarth, vaguely "arty" and with clearly defined ideas that brooked no nonsense. John and Nina Lang, as it has already been stated, lived in the top flat.

When they had first viewed their future home Nina had looked askance at the three flights of stairs, but the moderate rent and the large and well-lit studio room had proved so very attractive that John had signed a three-year lease and shortly afterwards they had moved in.

Each morning from Monday to Saturday at a quarter to nine John kissed Nina good-bye and hurried down the tree-lined road to the tube station that sucked the streams of workers down into its metalled throat, to cram them into packed trains rushing busily towards the City; and every morning Nina, watching her husband's black-clad back from the casement window as he started for his labours, was convinced that no young woman had a more enterprising, energetic and wholly satisfactory lord and master. There were not many men, she reflected, who within eighteen months had risen from a three- to a six-hundred-a-year salary. Once again she pondered this pleasant thought on the bright Thursday morning in early August on which this story opens.

Nina crossed to her writing-desk and salvaged paper and the

stub of a pencil from its chaotic contents. Two more days and they were to start their holiday. She ran over in her mind what they would need. For two glorious weeks they were to go for a walking tour in Normandy and they had determined to be as lightly burdened as possible. She quickly jotted down her own requirements, and drew a careful line. Then she wrote in neat printing the word JOHN. He would want three spare pairs of socks, a pair of slippers for the evening after a hard day's walking, tooth brush, shaving things ... gradually the little list grew ... oil yes, and a spare shirt. She liked the short-sleeved sports shirts —she would take him that evening to choose one. She thought that a bright blue would suit him. The sun blazed down on the quiet road and already the pungent smell of warm tar was noticeable. Nina put down her list and went to the small kitchenette to tell the daily woman, Mrs. Sparks, that she could clear away the breakfast and to give her the orders for the day.

Saturday morning found the flat a scene of some confusion. Tables and chairs were littered with discarded "essentials" that John had, with laughing ruthlessness, refused to take, declaring that a troop of baggage mules would be necessary to transport such an equipage rather than one frail man. At last with a pack of almost reasonable dimensions the Langs bade farewell to the interested Mrs. Sparks, and, hailing a taxi, drove to Victoria, from where they were to start their journey.

The crossing proved agreeable and the evening found them wandering round Havre, where they had decided to spend the night. A most satisfying hour was spent in poring over maps and in arguing the route which they should take. The next few days were uneventful, and it was not until Thursday evening that, healthily tired and extremely hungry, they arrived at the little village of La Bézard. The sun had lost its heat and an atmosphere of peace pervaded the little square, flanked on one side by an ancient and weather-stained church, in front of which a circular fountain of worn stone provided a seat for groups of gossiping housewives. Pigeons pecked industriously among the uneven cobbles. A few awning-shaded stalls stood in one corner of the square, their owners dozing on upturned boxes or stools; for most of their business had been conducted and the piles of vegetables and cheeses had for the greater part found their way into the baskets of their keen-eyed customers. The clock in the square tower struck seven, the deep notes very clear in the quiet of the evening.

"Shall we put up at the Hotel Royale?" asked John, brushing his fair hair back from his eyes and looking at the unpretentious inn, which, as far as they could see, was all that La Bézard boasted in the way of hostelries. Nina nodded. "Yes; oh, John, isn't this heaven? And look at those booths—it's just like a picture by Claude Monet."

She wandered over to the stalls. Immediately the proprietors lost their comatose apathy and, with the shrewdness of their race, prepared to do business with the foreigners that the good God had seen fit to send them. Nina passed the vendors of produce and paused before a great barrow piled with a collection of miscellaneous junk, wherein books, religious figures, bric-à-brac and cheap jewellery jostled each other in intriguing confusion. Immediately Nina was filled with the collector's acquisitive fever. She rummaged through the medley, finally selecting a small figure of "Our Lady."

"Darling, I think this might be old. Shall we ask how much this is? It looks like silver but it's so dirty it's impossible to be sure."

John let his pack slump on to the cobbles. Their combined French was fluent, if faulty, and they had none of the insular self-consciousness about airing it. The old man behind the barrow looked at them appraisingly. In answer to their query he replied "forty francs"—and then wondered if he had asked too much. From one of his usual patrons he would have asked "ten."

"Ridiculous!" Nina moved away.

"One moment . . . to Madame shall we say . . . thirty?"

Nina still contrived to appear disinterested.

"Well, for *Madame* . . . twenty—and you ruin me!"

They returned to the barrow. "I think it's worth that, darling," Nina said, "and it *is* rather charming." Meekly her husband handed over two tattered notes patched with stamp paper.

They approached the hotel. Only one more temptation stood between them and their goal. An array of gaily coloured cotton scarves, ties and shirts were heaped on two trestles covered by well-scrubbed boards. Once more Nina hesitated.

"I like those tricolour handkerchiefs—and they're only five francs each. Let's get one."

While their purchase was being wrapped up she caught sight of a number of belts coiled snakelike in a cardboard box. "Oh, John, you want a belt—you're always giving your trousers a nautical hitch." She pulled the box towards her. "Get this." She held up a broad leather belt. Heavy, and fully three inches wide, it was ornamented with steel studs and had a tiny shield let into the leather behind the buckle. It was of a kind worn by workmen and was well polished by much use.

"I can't wear a thing like that," John protested.

"Why not? It will give you a tough appearance—like a pirate or highwayman—eminently suitable for our vagabondage." She turned to the buxom peasant woman. "How much?"

"Twenty-five francs."

"That's absurd. Why it's not even new."

"But the leather is good, strong, there is a lifetime of wear still, in that belt. And the workmanship. Examine for yourself the workmanship."

"I'll give you twelve francs."

After some minutes' friendly haggling the belt changed hands for fifteen francs, and together the young couple made their way to the Hotel Royale, where they engaged a room, clean, but spartan in regard to comforts. After a dinner consisting of an omelette and veal they were joined by the owner of the establishment, who complained bitterly of the hard times, due to the fall of the franc to the detriment of such tourist traffic as came his way, and the inefficiency of the reigning government. In spite of a strong smell of garlic Nina found his conversation interesting.

"I think La Bézard is one of the most attractive villages we have yet seen. It is rare in these days to find such quiet and peace."

"Peaceful! In the name of God," ejaculated their host. "You should have been here yesterday. The place was crowded not only for the weekly cattle market, but also for the execution of that devil, Henri Larne."

John raised his eyebrows interrogatively and suggested another drink. The man lifted his replenished glass.

"Yes, he was a bad one! I myself hardly knew him, but Marie, my wife, is from his village and knew him well," he continued. "Big as a gorilla and strong as an ox and with a temper like a louse-ridden mother-in-law. Well, as I told you, he lived in the next village, Bierthieux, a few kilometres from here. Lived there with his wife and baby daughter, a little thing of three years she was. The wife, that unfortunate, no one knew how she stood him. When Larne had the drink in him he would beat her. It was a scandal. Then on a night in the spring when he had been drinking in the Red Flower he was boasting of his power over women. One of his listeners, Pierre Justand, lost patience with the braggart and told him to hold his tongue, adding that it was common gossip that his only daughter was by another man, so *phst* for his charm and powers! For that little one was the one child they had! It was a stupid thing to say and untrue into the bargain. Well, Larne went back to his cottage and beat and kicked his wife and the baby to death. And they executed him yesterday—nearly four months later. Yes, he was a bad one!"

The man wiped his moustache with the back of his hand and sighed. "And you say we are quiet here and peaceful," he ended cynically.

"What a horrible story," Nina said. "Poor woman!"

Nina turned from the fly-blown mirror and gave a final tug to the handkerchief that she had tied scarfwise round her neck. "Hurry up, John, I'm starving."

Her husband looked up from cleaning his razor. "I'm nearly ready." He picked up his belt from where it lay on the chest of drawers and drew it round his waist, pulling it tight and buckling it at the last hole.

"A little on the big side," he remarked with mock contrariness, as they went down to the little café to breakfast.

They had planned to make for the town of Balincourt that evening, but so great was the charm of La Bézard that Nina wished to stay over one more night and see the ruined château that lay a few miles to the south. Accordingly, provided with sandwiches, they set out. The day was hot but dull, and neither felt inclined to talk. Plodding along by John's side Nina thought that he looked sullen, but decided not to question him. His usually cheerful face was frowning and his lower lip projected sulkily. The sky was overcast as if a storm was threatening. On their arrival at the ruins they ate their lunch. John's depression continued and he answered her attempts at conversation with monosyllables. A rumble of thunder growled in the distance.

After lunch, at which John emptied his flask, which, much to his wife's astonishment, since he was a light drinker, contained brandy, they decided to explore the château.

They were in what had been the kitchens of the vast twelfth-century building when, on looking up one of the huge chimneys, moss grown and ragged Nina heard the plaintive mewing of a cat. She peered up at the place from which the noise appeared to come, but could see nothing.

"John, darling, do you hear that cat? It's either hurt or frightened."

They retraced their steps and looked up at the frowning stones. Twenty feet from the ground and on a narrow jutting ledge Nina saw the frightened animal, its piteous complaint silenced as it gazed down at them with alarmed, amber-flecked eyes.

"We must get it down," Nina said. "It must have been there for days. Look, John, there it is."

She glanced up at John and was astonished to see his expression. He was smiling and looking at the animal as if pleased by its unhappy predicament.

"I'll get it down all right," he said. He picked up a stone and flung it at the cat. His aim was good and the little creature after a moment's wild scrabbling fell to the ground, where it lay arching in agony.

Nina was horrified. "John, you *beast*. How *could* you?"

She ran forward and knelt beside the cat.

"Oh, you've broken its back." A little moan escaped her lips.

She looked up at John, her eyes blazing. "I *hate* you," she said viciously.

He stood with his left hand tucked into the wide leather belt, a smile twitching the corners of his mouth. "Don't be so silly, Nina. It's only a stray." He bent down and, picking the cat up by its hind legs, swung its head against the wall. A little blood splashed Nina's dress as she knelt at his feet.

There was a second rumble of thunder; and a few drops of rain, soft and heavy as tears, fell on the cat's blood-matted fur as the storm broke.

At ten o'clock that night, when the Langs failed to return to the hotel, Jules Thieraud was troubled. The thunderstorm had been terrible, but it had spent itself by five and the château was only an hour's walk from La Bézard. After consulting his wife, they, together with his son-in-law, decided to form a search party. Those ruins were dangerous places . . . and in a tempest so furious!

The moon, softened by storm clouds of moss agate fragility, cast a fitful light as the tiny cavalcade threaded their way among the grass-covered courtyards of the château. Jules carried an old-fashioned lantern which swayed and flickered as he stumbled down the treacherous steps that led to the old kitchens. Suddenly Marie gave a faint cry. "There, Jules, by the chimney. . . . What is that?"

Huddled on the wet grass, her arms raised as if trying to protect her face, lay the body of Nina, her dress torn from her body, which was terribly cut as if a heavy whip studded with nails had torn through her flesh. As they bent over her, her eyelids fluttered. "John. . . ." The whisper was so faint as to be almost inaudible. "John. . . ." Once more her lashes flickered. Her face was cruelly bruised, brutally trampled by heavily booted feet. A few feet away lay the crushed body of a cat and a wide bloodstained belt, set with studs and a small shield.

"Look, Marie . . . it is the husband's belt . . . lying there, I noticed him wearing it this morning."

"Mother of God!" Marie bent to look, but fearful of touching it. "*Monsieur's* belt you say? . . . it belonged to Henri Larne . . . many times I have seen it. . . ."

Mrs. Sparks was astonished when she read the news in her Sunday paper. "Well, it only goes to show that one never knows," was her comment. "So happy they seemed, too! And such a pleasant-spoken young gentleman! Well I never! It makes me go goosey, so it does! Such an affectionate young couple, I'd have said! Another cup of tea, Mrs. Noggs? Yes, I did for them for almost two years and never for a moment . . ."

"I always knew there was something strange about those Langs," said Philippa Togarth to her sister. "If you ask me . . ."

The two young men met outside their communal bath. "See that that fellow Lang has bumped off his wife?" asked one. "Yes. Pretty little thing she was, too," the other answered. "After you with the bath, old boy."

The Treymaines gave no opinion, for, as a confused matter of principle, they never read the Sunday papers.

The leather belt was used in evidence, but there was never any doubt as to the outcome of the trial.

HAVELOCK'S FARM

The farm-house overlooked a weed-fringed pond, mottled with that yellow and green vegetation frequently found in stagnant water. A number of barns and outhouses surrounded the main building, while at the back an orchard sloped sharply away down the hillside. The house itself had been built towards the end of the fifteenth century, and the bricks had taken on the exquisite soft red that only the passing of many years can give. In the evening the glory of a brilliant sunset would flame in the glass of the windows, forming a blaze of rich colour that was arresting in its beauty.

Havelock's Farm had been in the possession of the same family since the day that it had been built. The Havelocks were an odd people living away from the rest of the village, playing no part in the life of the community. For generations they had intermarried with other Havelocks from the neighbouring hamlets of Garth and Stoneley Bridge—dark, beetle-browed men and women, sturdy with the strength of the soil.

Leaseley, where the farm was situated, numbered four hundred souls—the Appins, the Furrowes, the Cartrights, the Masons, the Berries. In the way of remote country districts, it was rare for a new name to make its appearance. Brides, it was true, married into Leaseley, bringing new blood, but the influence of the five families had always remained unchallenged.

As has been said, the Havelocks moved in a different orbit from this little world—tilling their land, tending their cattle and sheep, meeting their neighbours only on market days. "Aye, the Havelocks be a funny lot," the people of Leaseley would say. "If they want no truck with us that won't make us fret at nights." The children indeed were brought up to look upon the Havelocks as a clan apart, feeling for them a queer mixture of fear and mockery.

With the passing of the years it was found necessary to engage a second teacher to help the old man who taught in the tiny school at the bottom of the hill; and a new classroom was added to the original structure. It was for this reason that Faith Harrison was sitting, surrounded by bags and boxes, in the ramshackle cab that had met her at Chartwell station and that was now bumping her over the seven miles of uneven road to Leaseley.

She had been informed that she was to take charge of the twenty children that comprised the "infant" class. The salary was small, but in view of her youth, the position was acceptable, rather for the experience than for the remuneration. Small in truth, for this was according to the standards of nineteen hundred and eight.

It had been after five o'clock when Faith had left Chartwell, and on her arrival at Leaseley she was surprised to find that three-quarters of an hour had passed in the venerable vehicle. She directed the driver to Shirley Cottage, the address that she had been given. With much ado the ancient Jehu helped her with the luggage, then, with a curt "good night" he turned his cab and clip-clopped away into the dusk.

Forlornly, Faith walked up the uneven flower-fringed path. A lighted lamp glowed behind heavy green curtains. She knocked at the door a little timidly. The shuffle of slippers, slithering on a stone floor, came to her ears. The door was opened by an old man not, Faith considered, over particular as to his personal cleanliness.

"Does Miss Parsons live here?"

"No. But my name is Parsons. I'm the schoolmaster."

The girl was very much taken aback by this answer.

"But I thought my superior was to be a woman, and that I was to lodge with her."

The old man smiled. "And I, my dear young lady, was under the impression that my assistant was to have been a young man. There must have been some mistake. But come in and have a cup of tea. I'm making some for myself at this moment. No," he added as Faith turned towards her luggage, "leave that where it is until we can decide what is to be done with you."

Faith followed him into the sitting-room, where a fire was burning. Her host busied himself with the teacups, adding a second plate to the ready laid table. "My name," he said again, "is Joseph Parsons, and I am known to the children as 'Dirty Joe' —nasty little brats."

Faith was surprised to find that she was liking this strange old man. She sat down in the armchair by the fire and gratefully sipped the hot tea that was handed her.

"And now we must see what is to be done with you," he continued; "obviously you cannot stay here. In the first place, I have no room—the young fellow would have had to share mine—and in the second place, it would not be at all decorous. No . . . we shall have to find you lodgings in the village until the mistake is rectified. When you have finished your tea we will walk round and see Mrs. George Appin. She is the village busybody and will be sure to know where we can find a bedroom for you."

But Mrs. Appin did not prove at all helpful. They discovered her sitting on a stool behind the counter in the general store that she owned and which was the sole shop that Leaseley possessed. She looked up in surprise as Joseph Parsons and the girl came in. It was most unusual to see a stranger.

"Good evening, Mrs. Appin. This is Miss Harrison who is to be my assistant. I wondered if you knew of anybody who could put her up, until she gets settled."

Mrs. Appin extended a plump hand to Faith. "Pleased to meet you, Miss Harrison, although I'm sure that I don't know anyone in Leaseley who could take you in. Fair bursting out of their houses as it is. We're a productive lot in Leaseley. Ten of my own I've got, and never lost a one! Now if you was to ask in Garth perhaps you would be luckier. Garth be six miles from here. But there—that would be too far, I'll wager. You poor thing, whatever will you do? A shame sending you here and nowhere to lay your head. Ah well, we all have our difficulties! As I was saying to George only yesterday . . ." Mrs. Appin broke off as a gaunt black-haired woman entered, closing the door behind her. "Good evening, Mrs. Havelock! It's not often we have the honour of seeing *you* in the village," she said with heavy sarcasm.

Mrs. Havelock made no answer but put down the string bag which she was carrying on the counter.

"And what can I have the pleasure of obliging you with?" Mrs. Appin continued in the same tone.

"A dozen candles and two pounds of lump sugar," the woman answered.

While Mrs. Appin was attending to these wants she kept up a running flow of condolence to Faith and Joseph, purposely ignoring the new customer.

"No, I don't rightly see what there is to be done. It's too late to go back to Chartwell now, *and* it looks as if it will be foggy later. Whatever will you do?" She gave a practised twist to the blue paper bag containing the sugar, and turned to get the candles. "It's too bad. But, believe me, you'll never find a lodging in Leaseley, search how you may. Here you are," she added, handing the packets to Mrs. Havelock. She pocketed the money that her customer extended and gave her twopence change.

The woman turned without a word and went towards the door. With her hand on the latch she paused, then addressed herself to Faith.

"You're wanting a lodging? Will it be for long?"

"I don't quite know. There seems to have been a great muddle. I'm Mr. Parsons' new assistant teacher, and he thought I'd be a man, and I thought he'd be a woman, and now we're not, and I've no place to go." The girl finished breathlessly.

Mrs. Havelock seemed in no way bewildered by this confused explanation. "Well, I daresay we could find room for you at the farm if you're so minded, and are willing to pay prompt."

Faith sighed with relief. "Oh, that is kind of you. I left my luggage at Mr. Parsons'. You see I thought I was staying there, and ..."

Mrs. Havelock cut her short. "I'll send Tom down for it after supper. Will you come along now or later?"

"I think I'll come with you, if that's alright," Faith answered. She had no fancy for a lonely journey in the dark tree-shrouded roads. She turned to Joseph. Mrs. Appin stood silent, her mouth pursed in disapproval, her silence pregnant with unuttered condemnation of Mrs. Havelock, her ideas and everything appertaining to her.

Havelock's Farm was situated about half a mile from the last house of the village, at the top of a steep hill. Faith had had a long day and was already tired out when they started on their way. By

the time that she had toiled to the summit she was out of breath,
being unaccustomed to hard walking. Her companion was unaf-
fected by the climb. The walk had been undertaken in silence,
and Faith was grateful that she had arrived at her journey's end.
Mrs. Havelock preceded her into a small square hall, devoid of
ornament, its plastered walls bare. Two massive doors led to the
living-rooms, a third gave on to the staircase leading to the upper
story.

Mrs. Havelock opened the door on the left, and, motioning
the girl to follow her, went into a long, low-ceilinged kitchen.
The table was laid for supper. Faith was subjected to a close scrutiny by the five occupants. Mrs. Havelock crossed to the dresser
upon which she placed her purchases. Then only she found it
time to explain the girl's presence. The other members of the
family made no comment on her addition to their circle, con-
tenting themselves with a slight nod as acknowledgement of the
introduction.

"My husband Tom . . . my daughter Millie. . . . That's Grannie
there in the corner . . . my son Abel . . . and his wife, Lucy. That's
the lot of us but Tom's brother Edward—and he's out yet. Set
another place, Millie. Miss Harrison, you'll find we live rough
like, I'm afraid."

Faith smiled her satisfaction with these preparations. She felt
swamped by this dark, dour family. They sat down to supper,
Faith being placed between Mrs. Havelock and Abel. With dis-
patch her hostess served out the stew from a great bowl in front
of her. By each plate there was a large hunk of white bread. The
meal was eaten with the minimum exchange of words. Cheese
and onions followed, and cups of strong brewed tea.

"Millie, keep your Uncle Edward's hot—he should be back
soon. And now, Miss Harrison, perhaps you'd like to see your
room?"

Faith followed her up the staircase to a back room lit by a single
uncurtained window. The ceiling on one side sloped sharply to
within a foot of the floor.

"I hope you don't mind the window being on the small side,
Miss Harrison. The bars were put in when my son Simon was a
boy." She hesitated, "He doesn't live in the house . . . any longer."

Then added more briskly, "You'll be tired no doubt, and would like an early bed. Breakfast is at seven. I'll be leaving you this candle. You can stay here for a week or two if you're so minded. Eight shillings and sixpence a week, with your breakfast and supper. Good night," and Mrs. Havelock closed the door sharply behind her.

Left alone, Faith shivered. The bed was narrow and the one sheet and blanket appeared but poor protection against the chill night air. Downstairs she heard a door slam.

"That must be Uncle Edward," she thought to herself. Slowly she began to undress, and made a perfunctory toilet in the wash-basin in the corner; then, putting her coat on the bed for additional warmth, she slid between the coarse, cold sheets and blew out her candle.

The moonlight lay like a band of bent silver across the floor and over her clothes folded neatly on the wooden chair.

"Dirty Joe" had dispatched a letter to the authorities explaining the incidents of Faith's unexpected arrival at Leaseley; but so slowly do the wheels of officialdom revolve that the days passed without any steps having been taken.

In the meantime she had taken up her duties in the school, duties which she found a great deal easier and less irksome than she had expected.

She saw little of the Havelocks. A hurried breakfast—and she set off to begin her day. When the work was finished she was in the habit of taking tea with Joseph or Mrs. Appin. The latter showed an avid interest in the life at the farm, but was disappointed in finding her new friend ignorant—or maybe reticent—on that absorbing topic. On her part, however, there was no lack of conjecture and hints as to the character and reputation of the family in which Faith lived. Inbreeding, she said, had made the Havelocks "not quite right." "Mind you," Mrs. Appin declared, "I'm not saying they're daft—but there's bad blood in that lot. Otherwise why should they be so secretive? And that Tom and that Edward—they're properly simple, or my name's not Mary Appin!"

Edward Havelock, who appeared to be the especial target of Mrs. Appin's distaste, differed from the other members of his family, by reason of his extreme good looks. In the late thirties, he was some ten years younger than his brother Tom. An inch under six feet in height, he had a well-built and muscular body, kept in perfect condition by his arduous manual labour. He had, in common with the others, the jet black hair of the Havelocks, but where they had brown eyes, his were of a deep blue. From the first he had, in his incoherent manner, tried to make himself agreeable to Faith. Such behaviour drew down upon him, and upon the object of his chivalry, the disapproval of his relatives who, while tolerating the stranger in their midst, had no wish to keep her there indefinitely.

One evening, when Faith had been at the farm nearly two weeks, Edward crossed the room to where she was sitting by the fire and offered to hold the wool which she was using in her work. Flattered by such well-meant attention Faith showed him how to dip his thumb and keep the wool taut to facilitate matters. As they were engaged in this domestic occupation—the man incongruous in his stained corduroys and muddied leggings—he leant towards her and said:

"There's no need to be frightened, Miss Harrison, he be alright really, and if you meet him kindly there's no call for alarm."

Faith could not understand what he meant. She was about to elucidate this saying, when Mrs. Havelock, who had been regarding them with her bold bright eyes, joined them and, with a sharp "You're too clumsy, Edward, for such woman's work," ousted him from his position and herself finished the wool winding. Such blatant intervention could not but increase Faith's suspicions that something out of the ordinary existed in the life at the farm; but since Edward never again referred to the conversation, and she herself hardly cared to do so, she tried to convince herself that it was meaningless, and that her imagination was conjuring up bogies without existence.

Still, the mystery in which the Havelocks were shrouded did little to reassure her in this commonsense belief.

Despite the absence of luxuries at Havelock's Farm, the schoolmistress was never allowed to help in the running of the house. If hot water was needed, or if on especially cold nights the girl asked for a fire in her room, it was always Lucy or the mistress of the house herself who brought these necessities. Faith was as ignorant of the storehouses and barns as she had been on the evening of her arrival. One night, however, she woke, her throat dry, and on finding the water-jug empty, she lit her candle and ventured down to the kitchen, closing her door gently so as not to rouse the sleeping household.

She was crossing the flagged floor of the kitchen towards the scullery door when a slight noise made her pause, and turning, she saw Mrs. Havelock watching her intently. A worn tweed coat covered her night attire and her feet were bare.

"What are you doing? What is it that you want?"

"I'm sorry if I disturbed you," Faith answered, "but I was thirsty, and as my water-bottle was empty I came down to get a drink."

Mrs. Havelock looked at her closely before replying.

"That's Lucy's fault. I'll speak to her about it in the morning."

She took the carafe from Faith's hands and filled it at the tap in the scullery.

"And the next time you're lacking anything just give Lucy or myself a call and we'll get it for you. There's no need for you to go trapsing round the house at all hours. You'd be wiser to stay in your bedroom, Miss Harrison. I'll thank you to remember that!"

Faith followed her back to her bedroom feeling extremely chastened, like a child caught in a serious misdemeanour. She was uneasy—more than ever convinced that the Havelocks were concealing something. Their shadows, made monstrous by the wavering candle flames, danced in crazy pantomime on the wall behind them.

The wind had risen when, two weeks later, Faith locked the door of the school behind her. All day long the windows had rattled under the assault of gusts of increasing violence. Great masses of black clouds raced across the slate-grey sky. As yet the rain held off. The lanes were carpeted with leaves stripped from the trees. The blustering October wind worried the branches to give up their coverings. Whirls of leaves spiralled into the air, slanting suddenly to the earth, where they whispered and scuttered on the hard surface of the roads. Anxiously Faith glanced up at the heavens. She decided to return to the Farm immediately. With lowered head she went forward, gasping a little at the force of the resistance she encountered. As she reached the hill-top the first drops of rain stung her face.

After supper she went to her room, taking with her a bundle of exercise books that had to be corrected by the next day. The Havelocks had been even more silent than was their custom. Faith had the impression that they were frightened of the rising storm. It seemed an absurd idea, she had thought, looking around at their brooding faces. As early as she considered possible with graciousness, she went up to her room, intending to read and work until she was tired. An hour later she got into bed and lay watching the lightning play behind the dark masses of the buildings and trees.

After a time she slept, a dream-haunted slumber from which she was frequently awakened by a thunderclap of unusual violence.

At length she gave up the unequal struggle and, slipping into her quilted dressing-gown, pulled up a chair by the window to watch the full fury of the storm. A vicious fork of lightning appeared to strike the big barn to the left of her point of vantage. She sprang to her feet in alarm.

For a few moments nothing happened, then she heard the slam of a door. The hurrying of feet in the passage. Mrs. Havelock's voice: "Lucy, stay in your room. . . . Edward, Simon's got out. . . . Abel, hurry downstairs at once. Gort's barn's been struck . . . Simon's free, I tell you. . . . I'll see to the girl. . . ." Then came the noise of feet speeding to the staircase, muttered questions. Then the voice of Tom: "For God's sake, Linda, what shall we do, now?"—and Mrs. Havelock's answering "Coax him into the woodshed. Quick, now!"

Faith heard the scrape of a key turning in the lock, and knew that she had been imprisoned in her room. Bewildered, she turned back to the window. The rain was falling in a solid sheet. Every few seconds the yard was thrown into brilliant relief by the lightning. As she looked she saw a man dart from the direction of Gort's Barn; and at the same moment heard the crackling of fire. The thatch had caught alight, and soon the flames glowed redly through the murk. Abel ran by with Tom, both men carrying heavy sticks. For a time the yard was deserted, then the figure she had seen reappeared; the other men in close pursuit. The unknown quarry, she perceived, was bearded, and waved a piece of blazing timber in his hand. He was cornered against the wall of the woodshed. She heard Tom shout: "Get him, Abel, we must get him—the madness is on him." They circled warily round the stranger who lunged at them with his fiery weapon. At a sign from Abel, the two men made a concerted attack. Faith could not see what was happening. Then the bearded man escaped from the mêlée, and, still carrying his crude torch, dashed into the house. The struggle in the yard was over. Tom and Abel picked themselves up and peered into the raging night. Clad in her shift Mrs. Havelock dashed from the house, her hair streaming behind her, the rain-soaked garment plastered to her body. With a low cry she ran to where the two men stood.

"Simon!—what have you done to Simon ... to Simon—my boy—my boy?" her wail was caught up by the wind. Tom pointed to the house and his lips moved. The girl saw their upturned faces. Mrs. Havelock was gesticulating. Together with the men she hurried back into the house. There followed the noise of great activity. Doors banged—murmured questions and answers and whispered instructions showed that an organised search was in progress.

Faith was beginning to feel frightened. She tried the door handle but found that she was still a prisoner. Lucy's voice shouted something—Faith thought she heard the words "on the roof." Footsteps scurried by her room. Returning to the window, she was in time to see Edward turning the corner by what she now knew to be the woodshed. He glanced up and a look of horror passed over his face. He cupped his hands to his mouth. "Tom," he bellowed, "he's up there, on the roof ... he's set the place afire!" Excited shouts greeted this information. The whole family gathered in the yard in an agitated knot. Their arms waved and they shouted instructions and threats to some one above the room where the girl sat. A trail of brilliant sparks blew from the eaves and was quenched by the rain.

The spectators below, as if by a common impulse, streamed back into the farm.

Faith flung up the window. The gale caught her by the throat. "I'm locked in. Let me out."

Her arms stretched out through the iron bars. For what seemed to her eternity, there was silence. Then came a banging on her door and Edward's voice.

"Are you there, miss? Open the door. Open the door. It's Edward. . . . Open the door. The whole building's burning like tinder."

As he spoke a wisp of smoke eddied through the hinges.

"I can't—they've locked me in. I haven't got the key. Fetch your mother—quickly, quickly."

The crackling of burning wood vied with the roar of the wind.

"No, don't. Come back," the girl cried. "Don't leave me—try and break the door down."

She could hear the jarring impact of his body; but the farm was massively built to withstand the centuries—as well to try and shatter a sheet of steel! The smoke grew thicker. She heard Edward's laboured breathing.

"I can't do it, miss."

"Then find Mrs. Havelock—the key—for God's sake." She heard him stumbling away. Shortly he returned.

"The stairs are ablaze. God help us both."

Faith ran back to the window. Plumes of burning thatch streamed in the wind. Shouts and cries echoed in the distance.

Edward renewed his assaults on the door. Suddenly, in the tumult of noise, Faith was aware that something was different—Edward had ceased his onslaught. Through the lintel she glimpsed the flames. The heat was becoming unbearable. She banged against the solid oak until her hands bled—attacked it vainly with the chair. A tongue of flame licked its inquiring way into the room. The ceiling above her was darkening. Fascinated she watched the charring beams turn from black to a dull, then a glowing, red. A shower of sparks fell on to her bedding. . . .

The scorched beams of the ceiling broke. Faith recoiled to the furthest corner of the little room. A crash, and a heavy body fell to the floor, moaning in agony. Horrified she recognised the bearded Simon. Terribly burned, he writhed in torture. Blazing wood and thatch showered into the room. Rearing on to his knees the wretched man extended blistered arms to the girl in a mute entreaty to help. There was a pungent sickening stench of burning flesh. . . .

The destruction of Havelock's Farm was seen for miles around. By the time help arrived from the village the ancient buildings were raging furnaces.

Four lives were lost that night. Mrs. Havelock in a last despairing effort to save the son, whose existence she had fought to keep a secret from all but her family, was buried in the ruins when the stairs collapsed. In life they had been together and in death they were not divided.

THE HARLEM HORROR

Michael Harwood walked quickly along the platform. All around him were people, pushing, jostling—making sure of getting their seats in the train. Yes—he could just do it. He ran the few steps to the sliding door, and stepped inside as they were closing. There was a moment's pause, and then the train slithered into the black hole of the tunnel. Michael looked at the rows of tired faces of the passengers opposite him. Lord! how he hated the Underground. He opened his paper, and glanced at the headlines.

MYSTERY OF SCIENTIST'S DISAPPEARANCE
SIR JOHN TROWBRIDGE NOT YET FOUND
LADY TROWBRIDGE INCONSOLABLE

and then, lower in the column in angry black letters

WHAT ARE THE POLICE DOING?

He turned over the page. He remembered the case. It had filled the newspapers for the last week. Sir John Trowbridge—perhaps the most brilliant surgeon of the day—had walked out of his house some ten days previously, and had never since been seen.

Michael pondered what could have happened to him. Amnesia had been the popular theory. He turned the page . . .

ACTRESS ROBBED IN HYDE PARK

Michael looked up, the train was running into a station.
"Oxford Circus."
Briskly he rose to his feet and hurriedly left the train. He was late, and anxious to get home.

Six months later Michael stood on the deck of the ss. *Gigantic*. He stood spellbound, gazing at the wonder that was New York's skyline. The dream buildings shot up in arrogant splendour as if to probe the secrets of the sky itself. The towers of the most amazing city in the world, Michael thought, a city that in the last hundred and fifty years had sprung from a humble Colonial town. Yet a city with a black record of crime and mystery. Only recently the world had been horrified at a series of inexplicable disappearances of children from the crowded suburbs of New York. During the last three months no fewer than eight children had vanished; vanished as completely as if the earth had opened and swallowed them, leaving no trace. In every instance they had been members of poor families—and had last been seen playing in the streets. The American police had done their best, no line of inquiry had been ignored, but nothing had been discovered. There had been a panic among the mothers of the districts, and a national outcry for some solution. Then, after a discreet interval, the matter had been dropped, and the disappearances had taken their place among the unsolved mysteries of recent years.

The morning promised great heat; for it was early July, and New York was experiencing one of its blazing summers.

And now Michael was to set foot in New York for the first time; the gangways were being put into position, the passengers were bustling to and fro in their eagerness to be the first ashore, and the liner was the scene of great activity. The docks were crowded with people meeting friends and relatives—handkerchiefs were fluttering—questions and answers were shouted eagerly by those on deck and those who waited for the moment when offi-cialdom should permit passengers to leave the liner. Michael felt aloof, as he looked at the smiling faces and gesticulating figures of his companions. New York seemed foreign—far more so than France or Germany.

"Isn't it marvellous, darling?"

Penelope, his wife, put her hand on his coat-sleeve. She smiled up into his face.

"I'm glad you like it," Michael laughed; "we're going to be here for the next three years, you know."

"I'm going to love it, I know I shall."

"We can go now, darling, if you're ready. Shall I carry Clare?" Penelope glanced at the child at her skirt.

"Yes, do, Michael. Isn't it a pity she's not old enough to remember this?"

"Well, she'll remember leaving it—she'll be nearly nine by the time we go home."

They were struggling towards the nearest gangway.

"Oh, Michael—isn't this all exciting!"

Michael squeezed his wife's arm. They were very much in love —and this America *was* just a little alarming.

Over two years had passed since that day when Michael and Penelope arrived with some hesitation on the threshold of New York. There was only a week until Christmas, and all the shops were bright with special displays—great electric signs bewildered the eye with their brilliancy, and crowds battled on the sidewalks, gazing in admiration at the store windows, or thrusting their way through the parcel-impeded throng into the stores themselves.

Michael walked slowly. He really must think of something to give Penelope, something that she would really like. Clare was no problem—children were easy to please. But Penelope....

He stopped in front of a window filled with lingerie and stockings made apparently from gossamer. No, he decided, clothes weren't exactly a "holiday" present. The next shop was a jeweller's, and suddenly he saw what he wanted. A ring. It was a large aquamarine, mounted in platinum. He went in and asked the price. Two hundred dollars, the sales girl said, and a bargain at the price! It was rather more than he had wanted to pay—but after all it was Christmas, and only that afternoon a letter had come from the Head Office in London, saying that the directors were very pleased with his work, and that promotion was waiting for him on his return.

And that was—in just over a year.

"Thank you, I'll take it."

He laughed as he thought of Penelope's pleasure. Seven o'clock. He hadn't realised it was so late ... and they were dining early and going to Radio City.

Penelope met him at the door of their furnished "apartment." She looked worried.

"Michael! The most terrible thing has happened. I tried to get you at the office—but you'd just left. Clare is lost—oh, what can we do?"

"Penelope—what do you mean? She can't be lost."

"I'm nearly off my head. I came in about six o'clock, and was just going to fetch her from Sally O'Brien's, where she was having tea—as you know, it's just at the end of this block—when the telephone rang. It was Sally, who told me not to bother to come, as Clare would come back by herself. There are no streets to cross, so I told myself not to coddle the child. I said I'd go and meet her. Well—I went, and I couldn't find her. It only takes two minutes from door to door, and Sally says she can't understand how I missed her. She's as upset as I am. I'll never forgive myself if anything has happened to her. Never. Never."

Michael ran his finger round the inside of his stiff white collar.

"Darling, what could have happened to her? It's not your fault, sweetest. Tell me—what did you do then?"

"I told the nearest policeman what had happened, and he telephoned to headquarters." She was crying with choking, gulping sobs. "And he said that they'd find her in no time. And then I telephoned you, but you'd left."

"But, Pen, that was over an hour ago. Haven't you heard anything since?" Michael's eyes were worried, the line of his jaw very hard.

"No—nothing."

And they heard no more that night, nor the next day. In fact, Clare had disappeared just as if she had never existed.

It was a sad Christmas for the Harwoods. Penelope, languid and worn with ceaseless grief and worry, refused to be comforted. Michael spent his days trying to discover some clue, however slight, to put the police on the trail of the kidnappers—for such an explanation was, to his mind, the only reasonable one.

And then, as time went on, they ceased to feel tearing, rending sorrow, but a dull grief was always in their hearts. Penelope refused to keep anything that reminded them of Clare. Not even a photograph was allowed to remain. But, unknown to her, Michael carried one in his pocket-book, and sometimes he would look at it, and remember all the vivid frail beauty of his lost child—her fair hair, her wonderful topaz-coloured eyes fringed with dark lashes. They were so unusual that even strangers had stopped to exclaim at their beauty; he thought of how, on the boat, Clare had been by far the loveliest child. He wondered if he and Penelope would have more children. Nothing else, he knew, would banish that look of hopelessness from her face. She seemed frozen, in a trance. There had been a telegram of condolence from Sir James Wood, the head of his firm: "My most sincere sympathy, if there is anything I can do cable me." But what could he, or anyone, do?

Of course, Michael realised, he was lucky. Damn lucky; he had his work, and so could forget—sometimes. But Penelope . . . he had suggested her going home to England, but she had replied: "Does it matter where we are . . . any more?"

He turned to the pile of papers awaiting his attention. He was glad to see the work lying there on his desk.

Another sweltering July held New York suffering in its fiery grip. Michael had noticed at breakfast that morning that Penelope looked unusually washed-out. He was thankful that they were returning to England at the end of August.

It was a Saturday morning, and the office week finished at midday.

"Where shall we go this afternoon, darling?"

"A cinema?"

"Pen, my dear. In this heat?"

"They're very well cooled."

"Even so. I say, darling—what about Coney Island? We've never been there, and as we're going home so soon it seems a pity to miss seeing it."

"But think of the crowds."

"That will make it all the more fun." His face was eager. He was boyish in his enthusiasm.

"All right."

"I'll be back at one. Let's have a cold lunch—and start directly afterwards. Then we can come back early and go to a cinema this evening, if you still want to."

Three o'clock found the Harwoods climbing up into one of those gigantic motor charabancs that plied to Coney Island—the Fun Fair of the New Yorkers. They got the last two seats; sitting wedged among pretty shopgirls and typists gay in the light summer frocks, and escorted by leather-belted young men in flannel suits and straw "boaters." Laughter and talk filled the air.

"Any seats left?" a lovely young Jewess asked the conductor.

"Plenty—bring the family, too. Use your eyes, lady—try the next coach. Dames like that bore my pants off!" he added to no one in particular. With a jerk the charabanc moved away.

Coney Island beach was literally black with sweltering humanity. The myriad side-shows were doing good business. Switchbacks bearing their cargoes of shrieking passengers swooped up and down, "barkers" inveigled the passers-by into the side-shows, sellers of rock and peanut brittle were doing a brisk trade; the ice-cream soda bars were three deep in patrons.

The sun beat pitilessly down upon this scene of bustling pleasure.

Michael and Penelope followed the crowd. They threw darts at playing cards, were thrilled by the dangers of "The Wall of Death," drank ice-cream sodas.

And then the rain came. At first in big slow drops, then in a quick tattoo. The holiday-makers dashed for the nearest cover. Michael put his arm round his wife, "In here, darling. Quickly, or your dress will be ruined."

They pushed their way into a large stuffy tent; peering over the shoulders of the people in front.

"Fifty cents!" a blowzy woman tapped Michael's back. "Fifty cents to see the Freaks, sir," she repeated.

Michael fumbled for the coin in his trousers' pocket.

"Oh, Michael, how horrible, don't let's." Penelope turned to struggle out. But they were by now pushed some yards from the doorway, and could hear the downpour of the rain.

"They won't be too bad, darling. They're mostly faked."

Slowly they made their tour of the big tent—looking at its incredible denizens. The fat lady, her face inhuman in its stupidity; the living skeleton; the two tiny dwarfs.

They were stopped by a crowd in front of a small wooden enclosure. In front of it was a placard, on which was printed: "*The Missing Links: These extraordinary creatures are believed to be the only two remaining in the world to-day. At terrific expense we . . .*"

Michael couldn't see how it went on, but between the shoulders of two young men in their shirt sleeves, Penelope caught a glimpse of "The Missing Links." Their skin was dark brown, and leathery in texture, their heads distorted out of all semblance to a human being's. Their tiny eyes were lashless and red rimmed, and their limbs moved constantly, aimlessly. Faint clucking noises came from their twitching mouths.

"They're ghastly—take me out. I don't mind if it *is* raining."

Michael could see the flapped entrance of the tent a little way in front of him. Only one more "exhibit" remained. But their way was blocked, for this evidently was the star attraction.

A showman stood in front of a wooden pen similar to that containing the two monstrosities. He was addressing his gaping audience. A huge coarse-looking fellow, he was standing with his thumbs tucked into the wide leather belt that encircled his waist. Sweat glistened on his face and hairy arms.

"And now, ladies and gentlemen, you will see the world-famed 'What-is-it?' The only creature of its kind in the world to-day. The creature that has baffled the most famous scientists. Discovered in the forest of one of the upper reaches of the River Amazon it is believed to be unique. Medical men can give no explanation —they say it is a female, probably of under ten years of age. But a female of what? Man or Monster? See if any of you ladies and gentlemen can decide. I will give fifty dollars if any of you can give an explanation of this remarkable phenomenon." He paused to wipe his arm across his streaming forehead. "She's beautiful, isn't she? Any of you young men like to marry her when she grows up?" He grimaced at his audience. "She'd make a good wife."

Penelope and Michael found themselves pressed close to the pen's side. On a bed of straw sat the "What-is-it." Its hair was long and dark, its skin mottled with spots like a leopard's. Its fingers hung straight from the second joints. Ears it had none. One of its eyes was closed, the lids sewn together.

"This remarkable creature," continued the showman, "is

unfortunately completely dumb. But in a woman that's an advantage, eh?" He laughed lewdly.

"Go and shake hands with the ladies and gentlemen."

Automatically the creature got slowly to its feet.

It waddled towards the side where Michael stood. Its one eye of a remarkable golden colour was without intelligence.

"And now, ladies and gentlemen—photographs of the 'What-is-it' may be purchased at the door. Ten cents each."

The crowd surged towards the opening; and Penelope found herself once more in the fresh air. The rain had almost stopped.

"It was horrible . . . horrible. Michael, I think I'm going to be sick." Suddenly she began to cry.

"Let's leave this place. I'm sorry, darling, I didn't know they'd be as nauseating as that."

Their bus back to New York was almost empty; but they passed fleets of other charabancs going to the Island. Saturday night was the best night of the week. All the side-shows were full; and hundreds of thousands of dollars changed pockets.

Penelope stood in the sitting-room of the flat that had been their home for the last three years, the flat where she had known such unhappiness. Strapped trunks, and half-filled suit-cases cluttered the floor. She frowned slightly as she tried to think if anything had been forgotten—her fur coat and Michael's big woolly Teddy-bear coat lay across a chair ready for the voyage that evening.

At the thought of going back to England her heart warmed. And she had news for Michael—glorious news.

She heard his key in the lock, and the next minute he strode into the room, big and broad-shouldered; and she was in his arms.

"Excited, darling?"

"Aren't you?"

"You bet! What time is the baggage-man coming for the luggage?"

"At three o'clock."

"Oh, Pen, it's good to be going home, isn't it?"

"Michael!"

"Yes, darling?"

She pulled his head down to hers. "Michael, darling, I think I'm going to have another baby."

"Penelope—my sweet darling!"

He closed his eyes. They were leaving New York that night— and with New York he hoped that Clare's memory would gradually fade. They were going home, and now Penelope was going to have a baby, and they could make a fresh and happier start.

"Oh, Pen," he said again, and there was great joy in his voice.

Michael paid off the taxi at the docks and followed his wife. As he turned into the dark doorway of the customs shed a boy touched his sleeve. "Paper, sir? Horrible discovery in Harlem, sir."

Absentmindedly Michael took a paper and thrust a quarter into the boy's hand.

"Thank you, sir."

On the great liner *Atlantis* all was confusion. Flashlight photographs of celebrities making the trip to Europe intermittently dazzled the eyes. He asked a steward the whereabouts of their cabin.

Half an hour later, he and Penelope stood by the rail watching New York draw away from them. Her great turrets were outlined against a sky illumined by a thousand lights, their bulk pierced by countless windows, lending them glamour.

His hand felt something in his overcoat pocket. It was the newspaper he had bought before coming on board. He unfolded it. On the front page in staring black letters he saw the following announcement sprawled across the whole sheet:

HARLEM HORROR!
GHASTLY DISCOVERY IN SECRET SURGERY!
FOUR YEARS' OLD ENGLISH MYSTERY EXPLAINED!

Fascinated he read of how the police, acting on information supplied by neighbours, had forced their way into a house in a low quarter of Harlem, how they had been obstructed by a maniac who was subsequently identified as Sir John Trowbridge, the famous plastic surgeon who had disappeared from his home in London four years before; of the abhorrent scene that had met their eyes in the Laboratory, of the bodies of children, vivisected out of all semblance to the human form. Of how Sir John had babbled and boasted of his remarkable achievements, and of his success in selling his "productions" to fairs and freak shows. Michael felt the world reel. He remembered Coney Island, and the "What-is-it" with one vacant topaz eye. . . .

He did not notice that Penelope was reading the paper over his arm.

"Michael! Oh, God—those children! . . . you don't think that Clare? . . ." Her voice rose to a shrill scream.

"No, dear, no, of course not."

"But how can we ever know, how can we ever *know*? . . ."

Michael realised that he had to make his decision quickly.

"*I* know. Darling—I never dared to tell you, but Clare was run over . . . she never suffered, poor little thing. They took me to see her body. It was pretty badly mangled. There would have been no point in taking you."

At all costs Penelope must never never realise this supreme horror.

"But, Michael, my own child, and you never told me! You denied me the right of seeing my child for the last time." Penelope's voice was cruel in its cutting quiet. "I think I hate you for this. I shall always hate you."

The great liner ploughed on towards the open sea.

Michael said nothing. There was nothing to say. Only that Penelope must never *never* know.

A POEM AND A BUNCH OF ROSES

"Why—did—I come, why—did—I come? why—did—I come?"
The regular throbbing of the engine beat the words into Sally
Russell's mind as the dingy train rattled past the few stations that
lay between Natombre and the little village of Civennes.

She could not understand what could have prompted Madame
de Civennes to ask her to the Château. *Why* didn't she hate her?
She sighed and tried to put the question out of her head. Perhaps
it was because Margaret de Civennes was Spanish, and could look
at life from a more detached angle. Still, Sally could not imagine
any Englishwoman that she knew asking her dead husband's mistress to stay with her, however passionately she may have loved
him.

She got up and started to collect her luggage ... the next
station *must* be her destination. The man in the ticket office at
Natombre had told her it was the third stop after changing at
Treves.

Sally shivered as she climbed stiffly from the train on to the
small country platform. There were few passengers for the little
village of Civennes; and, as might have been expected in a lonely
hamlet of its size, there was no porter. A disobliging greybeard
carried out the duties of ticket collector and station-master; nor
was his task an arduous one. She looked up and down the platform. An old peasant woman, blurred by the dusk, was clamber-
ing from her third-class carriage, her form rendered shapeless by
many bundles and baskets. She waddled away into the murk. A
bitterly cold wind blustered down the narrow valley.

Sally shivered and drew her coat more closely about her. She
looked past the cluster of wooden sheds to the road. No sign of
a car to meet her. Really it was very inconsiderate of Madame de
Civennes. With a sigh, she climbed back into her compartment
and started to tug out her suitcases and golf clubs. The little train
gave a warning whistle; and panic-stricken the girl found herself
in a cascade of small luggage on the now deserted platform. At

the same moment the welcome beams of a motor-car's head-lights cut the gathering gloom.

Sally gave a sigh of relief. The discomfort of the journey in the small local trains, the interminable dallyings at the dull stations, the dirt and smuts, all were forgotten by the prospect of dinner and a hot bath—especially a hot bath—at the Château.

The owner of the car was walking towards her, followed by the ticket collector, roused from his lethargy by a few well-chosen phrases. He was extremely deferential. "The lady from the Château—a thousand pardons. Would Mademoiselle permit him to carry her luggage?" Mademoiselle most certainly would!

Margaret de Civennes shook hands with her guest. She was remarkably good looking in her well-cut tweeds. The severe fashion in which she wore her dark hair enhanced the beauty of her face—the small mouth, the large sorrow-haunted eyes. Hers was a masculine, rather hard beauty that most men found intimidating. This flashed through Sally's mind as she protested that she hadn't been kept waiting at all; that the train had only just left.

Together they walked from the station and superintended the disposal of the luggage in the capacious dickey of the Bentley. Sally drew her coat more tightly round her and turned up the fur collar as a protection against the wind. She shivered.

"How far is it to the Château?"

"Five miles. You poor thing; you must be frozen." She had but the faintest accent.

Margaret pressed the self-starter, and they started their drive through the valley, its bleak beauty softened by the twilight, to the Château Montnegre, a relic of the glory that was mediæval France.

Sally gasped with appreciation at her first glimpse of the Château. Situated on a hill, its strong harsh outline black against the cloud-ridden sky, it dominated the valley through which the road wound.

The car pulled up before great gates of wrought iron. Margaret pressed the horn. The harsh metallic cry sounded oddly out of place. A light showed in the cottage of the gate-keeper, and a bent old man tottered uncertainly into the glare of their lights. He carried a lantern of a pattern in use many years ago. His purblind eyes peered at his hands as he fumbled with the fastenings. He touched his cap as the car slid past and breasted the steep slope of the drive.

The vast building loomed before them; a seemingly solid mass of masonry, save where one room lighted by candles pierced its flank with eerie radiance.

"I'll leave you here," Margaret said. "Pierre will take your luggage. I'm afraid that you'll find it very uncomfortable. You see, I just live in one wing with an old woman to cook for me; and her son to do the heavy work. All other help comes from the village; so I must garage the car myself. The bell is on the right of the door," she added as she let in the clutch.

Sally pulled the bell. Far away she heard the jangle of its ringing. She felt dwarfed by the gigantic size of the door. The trees tossed their branches, tortured by the wind; on such a night, she thought, witches straddled their broomsticks, riding the gale to their Sabbath. She listened. No sound disturbed the quiet of the Château. She pulled the bell a second time. She thought how brave it was of Margaret de Civennes to live here by herself! Then came the sound of footsteps on a stone floor, unhurried and purposeful. And then silence; whoever was there was waiting, listening. She wrapped on the wood with her knuckles.

The rasping of heavy bolts promised that soon she would be in welcome shelter. With a last protest the massive door swung open. Sally stepped forward; and then paused in amazement. Before her stood the biggest man that she had ever seen. He towered above her, nearly seven feet in height, his tremendous shoulders almost filling the narrow stone passage. But it was his face that startled the girl. From a forest of beard the mouth hung half open; the small pig eyes were bleared with lack of understanding. She glanced at his hands, huge and hairy, with prominent knotted veins. The man looked at her, motionless, and without speaking.

"My luggage is outside. Could you bring it in, please." Sally spoke in halting French.

He made no move; but stared at her in abysmal stupidity. She repeated her order; and then added: "Madame de Civennes is garaging the car. She will be here in a minute."

The servant shambled past her and picked up her suitcases.

With a jerk of his head he motioned her to precede him.

Sally walked down the passage until she came to a lofty central hall. A few candles served to lessen its gloom. She could just see a wide staircase that mounted into the darkness above. Armour and the glimmer of marble shimmered where the light caught them.

The man put down her luggage and threw open a door on the right, showing the warm welcome of a log fire. Sally decided that she was meant to wait there for her hostess. Was the creature dumb? she wondered. She hurried to the blaze, gratefully stretching out her numbed hands to the fire.

Taking off her hat and coat she threw them on to a chair covered with wonderful tapestry, its rich colours toned down by the use of many centuries. The door opened and Margaret hurried in, her face glowing from the cold night air.

"I'm sorry I kept you waiting. But I see that you've made yourself comfortable."

"Yes . . . Madame de Civennes, who is that extraordinary man who let me in?"

"You mean Pierre? Oh, he's not as intimidating as he looks, child. He's dumb, poor fellow, and not overburdened with brains. But he's a marvellous servant. I did his mother a service once, and they're both devoted to me. I hope he didn't frighten you?"

"No. Not—exactly. But he was a little . . . unexpected."

"I should have warned you." She walked towards the hall. "But I'm sure that you'll be wanting a bath and a change. I'll show you your room. We dine, or rather sup, at nine."

Dinner helped to dispel somewhat the atmosphere of gloom. The food was simple, but well cooked. A delicious omelette, cold ham and a salad, and fresh fruit, followed by excellent coffee. The meal was prepared by Marie, Pierre's mother, a wizened crone of incredible age, who also waited upon them. Afterwards, they went back to the cheerful sitting-room for liqueurs and cigarettes. Sally was struck by the pale sad loveliness of her hostess, ten years her senior, who, a Russian cigarette between her slim fingers, sat on a low stool gazing into the fire. 'She is very beautiful,' Sally thought, 'with a hard brittle beauty.' Soon Margaret rose, glancing at the clock.

"Well, my dear, it's half-past ten. There's no reason to sit up late in Civennes. I want to get some colour into your cheeks before you go back to London. If there's anything you want, I hope that you'll let me know."

Sally followed her up to her room. The wind had dropped and, the moon being obscured by clouds, the night crept close to the walls of the Château. Sally had never experienced a feeling of such solitude. It seemed that only four people remained in the world: Margaret de Civennes, herself, Pierre and the wizened Marie.

Well, here was her room. She yawned, stretching luxuriously. A profound fatigue swept over her. Sleep and rest were what she longed for; and let to-morrow take care of itself.

The next day she and Margaret walked to the village, a pathetic straggle of cottages, a half-mile from the Château, behind which the Montnegre reared its sinister bulk. It was dusk when they returned. Sally was tired and hungry, but her day in the open air had given her a feeling of well-being. Her hostess smiled at her. "You see, I was right in asking you to come to visit me. You needed a change."

"I can't thank you enough. But I want to talk to you about it all. I don't quite understand why you're doing all this for me. . . ."

Margaret shrugged her shoulders impatiently.

"Why bring up old stories? The past is dead—it is dangerous to resurrect it." Her voice held an odd note.

Later that evening after their dinner, when the two women sat smoking, Sally determined to talk out the whole situation with Margaret. She was deeply touched by her kindness, and wished sincerely that it could have happened otherwise. But at the time she had not known Margaret; and so had violated no sense of loyalty. Sally lay curled up on a sofa. They had been discussing books; the quality of courage—abstract questions that could hold no personal element. Margaret studiously avoided all but abstract discussions. And now Sally felt the time had come to try and justify herself in the eyes of this woman. She threw away her cigarette, quickly swung her feet to the floor, and brushed back her thick fair hair.

"Madame de Civennes;—or Margaret—I may call you Margaret?"

"But of course."

"I want to explain to you about André and I."

"My dear!" Margaret looked at her with surprise; the tone of her voice showed only unutterable boredom.

"But I must. You've been so charming to me, that I feel such a . . ." she groped for a word, "such a cad."

"Who can help their feelings?"

"You see, it wasn't as if I knew you. I met André at a night club. I knew he was married, but thought, God knows why, that he was living apart from his wife." She broke off. "You loved him terribly, didn't you?"

"He was all my life."

"I loved him too. That's why it was so dreadful when it all happened. Oh, it was horrible. And the newspapers—they didn't spare me, you know. I suppose that you read that he died in my bedroom—that I was engaged to be married . . . well, it's finished my life, if that's any consolation."

"That is why I asked you here—so that you could get away from London, until . . . your pride heals."

Sally got up and walked over to the fire, leaning against the carved stone of the fireplace. She found it easier to talk where she could not see the eyes of her hostess.

"It seems strange telling all this to his wife, doesn't it?"

"Is a wife, then, such a terrible person?"

"Margaret! I loved André. I loved him, and he loved me. We couldn't help it, really we couldn't. I remember the last time he wrote to me; the evening he died. I was waiting for him to call for me to take me out to dinner. The bell of my flat rang; and I panicked because I wasn't nearly ready. I thought it was André; but it wasn't. It was a messenger boy with a great bunch of red roses and a note. And the note was a poem. It said:

> *'Time was when I loved not,*
> *And loving not, rejoiced in love.'*

That's all. But I shall never forget it." Sally spoke with difficulty.

"And now I've met you," she continued. "At first I thought I wouldn't come here; that you must hate me. You've made me look so small and petty. You're a great woman, my dear." She started to cry. Margaret crossed to her, smoothing her hair with her hands.

"Don't cry, child. We both loved André. It's finished now; there's nothing left that either of us can do."

As she undressed that night, Margaret felt that her heart was dead within her. Nothing mattered any longer. André had betrayed her more than she had realised. She felt that she could have forgiven any infidelity but that. He had given *her* poem, her most treasured memory of their early marriage to that silly little . . . tart.

> *"Time was when I loved not,*
> *And loving not, rejoiced in love."*

Margaret's face was set in misery as she climbed into bed. Well, she should pay for it; the common little fool with her cheap sentiment. She, Margaret, had wanted to see what it had been that had so fascinated André. There must have been *something* in the girl!

And she lay sleepless through the night, her brain working feverishly through the still hours. That girl, she should pay for stealing her memories. "We both loved him." How dirty it made everything seem.

On the Saturday, as they were walking up the drive that led up to the Château, Sally said:

"I've been here a week. I suppose I must go back soon. I can't just mark time for ever, can I? I think I'll go on Tuesday, if that will be all right for you."

"If you must go, there is no more to be said. You know that you can stay as long as you feel you care to. What is the hurry? Future engagements?"

"Oh no. Nothing like that. None of my friends know when I am coming back, or where I am, as a matter of fact. It's a queer feeling that no one knows what's happened to me. It cuts this visit off from the rest of my life entirely. An isolated interlude."

They walked on. The night was beautiful with stars. A gentle wind whispered in the branches of the trees that bordered the avenue.

"An isolated interlude," Margaret repeated softly.

Monday was a glorious day, one of those brilliant April mornings that come all too rarely. Sally sat in a cane chair on the terrace, overlooking the panorama of the valley, washed in wan yellow by the spring sun. She was sorry, in a way, that she was leaving so soon, and yet glad; for the Château frightened her with its forbidding aspect. And that nightmare couple! That evil old Marie! Several times during the last two days she had noticed the old woman giving her a venomous glance as if she were gloating over some obscene secret, she supposed it was because she was unable to conceal the horror she felt for her son. Pierre! He was no better than an idiot. Yes, on the whole she was glad she was leaving. She looked up as she heard someone approaching. It was Margaret, with a bundle of magazines and newspapers under her arm.

"These have just come from England. I thought you might like to see them. By the way, if you are still determined to leave tomorrow, perhaps you might like to go over the Château. You've only seen the wing I live in. It's rather interesting. Parts of it go back to the ninth century."

"I'd love to." Sally walked to the french window that led into the library.

"Of course it's in grave disrepair," Margaret went on, "but you can get an idea of what it has been."

They spent the morning in going through endless rooms and passages, majestic still in their decay. Heavy Chinese curtains of painted leather, ragged as the binding of an old book; wonderful brocade-covered chairs; glowing tapestries; tortuous winding stairs; carved wooden galleries. Sally was bewildered by the impressions that crowded on her brain. At last they returned to the hall. Under the great staircase a narrow arched door was let into the stone.

"Where does that go to?" she asked.

"To the cellars and dungeons. The rock is honeycombed with passages. I don't know them very well myself. Old Marie is the only living being who does, I believe. It's cold down there; and there's no lighting. They were put to nasty uses in days gone by!"

She laughed and led the way back into the library.

During luncheon Sally again felt the malignant presence of old Marie. She shivered. The old woman must be slightly crazy. Again she wondered how Margaret could bear to live here by herself . . .

Margaret de Civennes stood in the huge stone kitchen of the Château. Before her was Pierre, his face strained in the effort to comprehend what his employer was saying. Behind him his mother sat hunched in her rocking-chair, knitting, the twitching of her needles as insistent as the ticking of a clock.

"You have been a good boy, Pierre. It is time you were rewarded, is it not so? See, I have for you a present. Some brandy." Margaret pointed to a bottle, shrouded in cobwebs that stood on a table. "And that is not all. Drink, my friend. Make merry to-night, and perhaps there will be something more for you."

The old woman glanced up at Margaret, her eyes bright with evil understanding. Pierre's thick lips parted in a grin. He was repulsive in his ugliness.

"Marie. Come with me."

The woman followed Margaret into the passage.

"It is arranged. It will be to-night. See that he drinks well. We can manage it between us. She is not heavy."

The harridan made a clucking noise of acquiescence. Her poor Pierre! Well, it was time he had some fun. He was human, wasn't he?

Sally was sleepy. She couldn't understand why she was so exhausted. It must have been the liqueur that Margaret had insisted on her drinking after dinner. The room was blurred. Bed . . . she would go to bed. She was too tired to undress. Too tired . . .

Pierre was sitting by the table in the kitchen. A glass was in his hand; the bottle of brandy, half-empty, stood on the table at his elbow. His old mother was talking to him, slowly, distinctly.

"You understand, Pierre. The English girl. . . . You could love her, eh? Then do so. She is yours. She will marry you. That will be good, eh?" She peered into his face anxiously. The man looked up at her, his eyes narrowed.

"You understand, Pierre?"

His great head nodded.

When Sally awoke she felt cold; piercingly cold. She opened her eyes. She had been dreaming that she was being carried somewhere. Where was she? She lifted her head and looked around her. She was lying on a heap of straw on a stone floor in a circular room, hewn apparently from the rock, and with no outlet but a heavy wooden door. She raised herself on her elbow. What had happened, where was she? She focused her eyes on a torch that flamed in a bracket on the wall opposite to her.

Suddenly she saw that the door was opening . . . somebody was coming in. Who was it? God! it was Pierre. . . . She gave a cry . . . staggered to her feet.

At six o'clock the next morning Marie knocked on the bedroom of Madame de Civennes.

"Well?"

"It is done, Madame. My Pierre is strong and very determined."

"That is good. I will not forget you, Marie." She chuckled and went quietly out of the room. Margaret lay on her bed, fully dressed; it was early yet, and the dawn glimmered behind the stunted trees that feathered the mountains. She crossed to the window and parted the curtains. The sky was faintly pink. Margaret spoke to herself, her lips barely whispering the words "... *and loving not, rejoiced in love.*"

Later in the day Margaret passed through the arched door to visit her guest.

"Reason it out for yourself," she said. "You have ruined two lives—your fiancé's, and mine. It is only right that you should make what amends are in your power. Pierre is a good man —a little uncouth perhaps—but still, a good man. Owing to his unprepossessing looks the girls here will have nothing to do with him. You can make him happy and you shall make him happy. You will stay here in this apartment until I see fit to allow you greater liberty. I will give you more comforts and you shall be adequately cared for by Marie. Later, when you have borne Pierre a child, I will arrange that he will marry you. It is the custom of the peasants so to wed in this part of the country. Should you not prove capable of childbearing, then it is for Pierre himself to decide whether or not he will take you in marriage. For my part I think it likely that he will do so. I shall now leave you. Any reasonable request you make will be told me by your future mother-in-law." Margaret turned as she finished speaking.

"Why are you doing this thing to me?" Sally demanded. "In whatever way I have injured you ... I ... are you a fiend that you can condemn me to such a life?"

"You have condemned yourself. I invited you here to see if there was anything fine in you; to try and understand why André loved you enough to kill himself when you refused to go away with him. You are exactly what I expected—shallow and cheap. You wished for a lover. He is dead ... for André's sake I have found you another."

Sally heard the grate of a key. The thickness of the door deadened Margaret's footsteps as she climbed the worn stone steps.

OBSESSION

The banns had been read for the first time of asking; and many of the congregation in the church turned covertly to glance at the girl who sat by her mother in the third pew on the left-hand side of the aisle. Doris Carson was well aware of this sly scrutiny and, feeling that the expected maidenly blush was absent, studied the prayer-book in her hands with becomingly pious zeal.

The announcement of her forthcoming marriage to Henry Russell came as a surprise to no one among the worshippers; for the two had been more or less openly "keeping company" for more than a year; and the death of Henry's father six months previously had left him alone in the big farmhouse that stood among ploughland and pasture a mile from the village of Hartledean. The ladies of the village considered that Sarah Carson's girl had done very well for herself, and felt, somewhat enviously, that she was extremely lucky; for Quarry Farm was one of the most flourishing in the district, due, they admitted freely, to the unremitting work put into it by Henry and his father, who had not spared either themselves or the half-dozen labourers that they employed.

Henry had just passed his thirtieth birthday, and it was only natural, they comforted themselves, that he should want to take a wife; and if it couldn't be their Janet or their Mary or their Maud —then Doris Carson was a well-spoken and good-mannered girl —and, Christian charity once more implanted in their matronly bosoms, they shortly afterwards rose a little stiffly to sing that sprightly hymn, "All things bright and beautiful."

Following the announcement of his marriage, the young man had appeared more bashful than his bride. His face crimson, he had sat with his hands convulsively clutching his knees, his neck, bulging slightly over his high starched collar, dyed the same ruddy hue. Now, however, sensing that Doris and he were no longer the cynosures of all eyes, he joined in the hymn with vigour, and, it must be added, in a pleasing baritone voice.

Looking up with approval at his broad back, old Mrs. Weatherby from the Post Office noted his regained composure, and her face crinkled in a knowing smile. Well, well, Tom Russell's boy and Sarah Carson's girl to wed! Half dreaming, the cavalcade of the years slipped past in retrospect. Her own arrival in Hartledean as a young bride in . . . the old lady frowned in her effort to recall the date . . . it must be nigh on fifty years. . . . Yes, in the summer of 1860. . . . Sarah's father-in-law had been the beau of the countryside in those days . . . handsome John Carson. With a slight shock Mrs. Weatherby remembered that John had been buried nearly a quarter of a century ago in the sun-washed churchyard that she could see through the small leaded windows. Lost in her reverie she felt her niece tugging at her arm; and was dismayed to find that she alone of the congregation was standing . . . a lone figure in a sea of bowed heads. She flushed with embarrassment and abruptly sat down with a force that jarred her spine, darting as she did so, an angry glance at her companion.

It was the custom in Hartledean for the church people to linger outside the porch after Matins, and to exchange greetings and gossip with their neighbours; and this glorious morning was ideal for such pleasant intercourse. Mrs. Weatherby, her right hand, in its thin black glove, resting frail as a leaf on her buxom niece's prune-coloured sleeve, followed the throng through the arched door into the sunshine, where she joined the little groups that were gathering, growing, dwindling and dispersing, only to re-form sociably in some other spot. Mrs. Weatherby saw Mrs. Carson and Doris standing by the iron gate, centres of a group of women who were congratulating the girl and her mother. Slowly she made her way towards them. As she approached she heard Miss Bourne, the doctor's sister, exclaim in her staccato manner, "Such a surprise, Doris. I'm so pleased for your sake! Henry is a good man! So hard-working! So *lusty!* What a lucky girl! How pleased your dear mother must be! Charming Farm!" Here she caught sight of Mrs. Weatherby, and broke off to give her a smile of welcome and a gracious inclination of her head.

Mrs. Weatherby patted Doris on the shoulder. "My dear," she said, "you must be very happy." The girl smiled at her, and the old lady, touched by the radiance in her face, was reminded once more of another bride of fifty years ago.

"I am." Doris looked very sweet and fresh in her crisp print dress with its straggling design of cornflowers. Her eyes glanced past Mrs. Weatherby and looked to where Henry was standing near the church door, his dark head bared, laughing with a group of young men. Their congratulations were hearty enough, even if their jokes might have been a little crude; for both Henry and Doris were well liked in Hartledean. As she looked he turned and walked towards her, burly and prosperous in his Sunday suit of dark serge, double-breasted and buttoning high on his chest. Doris thought that he looked his best in his farmer's clothes; somehow the blue suit seemed to hamper his solid muscular body. She liked to see him in breeches, his shirt-sleeves rolled to the elbows of his tanned forearms. At his approach the covey of well-wishers twittered with pleasure and good wishes.

"And how will poor Bessie like having a new mistress at the Farm?" Mrs. Weatherby asked playfully. Bessie was a good-hearted but forbidding spinster of some sixty years, who had run the farmhouse for Henry since his mother had died.

"She'll stay. She likes Doris well enough." His voice was slightly burred with the soft West Country accent.

"She's a good soul and a good worker. We'll get along nicely together," Doris agreed. "You're coming back with mother for a bite?" she added.

"Is that all you've got for a hungry man?" A discreet ripple of laughter greeted this sally.

"Well, I mustn't detain you," Mrs. Weatherby broke in. "Gracious!" she exclaimed, as the clock in the square tower struck twelve. "How time flies to be sure. Good-bye, my dear. Good-bye, Henry," and attaching herself once again to the arm of her plump and silent niece, she passed through the gate and into the High Street, on which looked the prim and lace-veiled windows of her front parlour.

"Dear Mrs. Weatherby," Miss Bourne was saying, "so gallant! Won't give up! Marvellous for her age! Have to retire soon, I expect! Reads all our postcards, I'll be bound! The Post Office won't be the same without her!"

And so the chatter and joking continued on this Sunday morning, a June day in the year of grace nineteen hundred and twelve, in the tranquil Somerset village, where a young couple had become engaged to be married. Presently, urged by pangs of hunger, the churchgoers departed to their homes.

Doris and Henry sat on the sofa in Mrs. Carson's sitting-room. The good lady herself was in the kitchen preparing the "high tea" with which she was accustomed to end the Sabbath, tactfully leaving them alone. They had spent the afternoon most agreeably in walking by the river-bank, and in much dalliance among the shady copses that fringed the sluggish water. Henry looked down at the head with its brown hair that rested on his shoulder.

"Love me, Doris?"

"A little."

"Not more than that?"

"You know I do, Henry!"

"As much as this?" He bent his head to hers and kissed her for the hundredth time.

"Just about."

"More?"

The sound of Mrs. Carson's footsteps were heard approaching and, at a tactful cough from that thoughtful lady, Doris sat up and moved away from the young man. The door opened and her mother came in.

"Oh, Doris. . . . Joe Langley is here and wants to see you. I can't imagine what he has come for . . . he seems dreadfully excited."

"Joe Langley!" Henry exclaimed in surprise.

"Jealous?" his mother-in-law laughed.

He grimaced. Langley was the simple-minded son of a widow who lived in a cottage on the Wimblemere road.

"Tell him you're busy, Dot," he suggested.

"I can't do that. I must see why the poor boy has come. I won't be long." She got up and, smoothing her dress, followed her mother from the room.

Mrs. Carson paused at the door to say:

"Smoke if you want to, Henry."

Left alone, the young farmer filled his pipe. He smiled to himself at the memory of Mrs. Carson's mocking "Jealous?" A fine rival indeed . . . the widow Langley's idiot boy. He leant back, jingling the coins in his pockets, and watched the clouds of blue smoke fading towards the low ceiling of the room.

Doris found Joe waiting for her inside the door that led into the stone-flagged scullery. He appeared to be in a state of extreme agitation. His long red hands, protruding grotesquely from the short sleeves of his ragged coat, twisted the cap that he held. Thin almost to emaciation, he appeared more than his twenty-four years, strangely senile—with a withered look of old age that lay oddly on his vacant face. The nervous twitch that perpetually agitated his left eye and the corner of his mouth robbed him of all expression. At the sight of her he tried to speak, but so intense was his excitement that for some seconds the attempt was too great for him.

"Yes, Joe? Why did you want to see me?"

With a tremendous effort he blurted, "Is it true what they're saying?"

"Who? What are they saying?"

"That you're to wed Henry Russell?"

"Yes, Joe, it's quite true. Weren't you at church this morning?"

He ignored her question. Suddenly he turned away to hide his emotion. "You can't do it, I tell you. You can't do it."

Behind her Doris heard her mother laying the table, and realised that Joe was embarrassed by her presence. Perhaps he would explain himself more easily if she were alone with him. For greater privacy she closed the door between the two rooms.

"I tell you you mustn't. It's not right. You're all I've got. No one else but you has been kind to me. You're my girl, do you hear, you're mine. I know I never asked you to marry me, but I thought you knew." He stopped speaking, exhausted by such a long speech.

Doris was dumbfounded. True, she had always been nice to the boy. She had felt sorry for him, witless and misshapen as he was, the natural butt of the crueller element in the village; and he had rewarded her by a doglike devotion. She had an irresistible desire to laugh, but the blank misery of his beseeching animal eyes stopped her. What could she say to him? She put her hand on his arm.

"Joe . . . I never dreamt you felt like that about me; how could

I? But I'm afraid it's too late. You see, I'm engaged to Henry, and it would hurt him terribly if I threw him over. You understand that, don't you?" She spoke slowly, so that her words would sink in. "I can't possibly marry you now that I'm promised to Henry. I didn't mean this to be a shock to you. I thought that you knew . . . I thought everybody knew."

He remained silent, his face twitching. The ticking of the clock on the table seemed very loud. "I think you'd better go, Joe. I'm sorry."

"You can't do it. . . . You're my girl."

And then he had gone, and Doris faced the door that he had slammed behind him. She looked through the window and saw that a fine summer rain was falling. Poor Joe . . . she smiled a little sadly . . . of all the ludicrous ideas!

"What did he want, dear?" Mrs. Carson asked, as she went through the kitchen.

"Nothing, mother. He'd just heard of my engagement and he felt a little upset."

"Joe Langley upset! What impudence!" Mrs. Carson banged a sugar basin on to the table.

Doris told Henry of her interview, and, as she had expected, he was greatly amused, and slapped his thigh; his laughter echoing into the kitchen.

"The poor loon! Let me catch him saying a thing like that, and I'll tan his hide for him quick enough."

"No, Henry, you won't. It's pathetic, dear. Leave him alone."

"Marry you! The little runt!" Henry pulled her down on to his knee, and by the time Mrs. Carson came to tell them that supper was ready, Joe Langley and his concerns had been forgotten.

During the days that followed Doris saw little of the half-witted boy. Occasionally in the village she caught sight of him, sullen and quiet, mooning outside the Blue Boar, or wandering restlessly along the road that led to his mother's cottage. He seemed oblivious of her presence, but she felt that his gaze followed her whenever her back was turned.

One morning she was on her way to the Post Office when she came upon a mob of schoolchildren running and laughing from a narrow lane that joined the High Street by the shop of John Tinkler, the baker.

They were closely followed by the upright figure of Miss Bourne, indignation in every line of her bearing and in the parasol that she brandished in her hand.

"Good morning, Miss Bourne." Doris was curious to find the explanation of her friend's militant conduct.

"Good morning, Doris. Really these children! Of course it's his mother's fault for not keeping him at home! Horrid little savages! But it's common knowledge that she has always been a drunken good-for-nothing!"

Doris smiled polite inquiry; and the good lady hurried on, "They've been tormenting him again! Joe Langley! A crying shame! I found them pelting him with stones! One had struck him on the ankle when I arrived on the scene! It's not Christian! I shall speak to the vicar! But then, I suppose that boys will be boys!" She paused for breath.

"Poor Joe—where's he gone?"

"He made off over the fields like a frightened rabbit! Kinder to send him to an institution, I should say!" and Miss Bourne bustled away, her shopping bag held firmly in her left hand, her gay parasol tapping the pavement in irregular accompaniment to her step.

Henry, on the other hand, was less fortunate. True to his promise to treat Langley with kindly tolerance, he tried to ignore the boy's persistent dogging of his footsteps. When he had occasion to drive to the village in his smart trap with its fat, well-groomed pony, he was aware of the simpleton's scrutiny; in the lanes around his farm he was continually encountering the loose-limbed figure slouching in the shadow of the hedges. Once he had caught him near the house itself; and had warned him that if he found him trespassing on his land again he would give him a sound thrashing.

After that Joe had been more circumspect in his shadowing, and nearly two weeks passed before his next meeting with Henry.

The young farmer was walking down the narrow path that divided a big field of wheat that lay some distance from the house. The hot sun of June beat down upon his bare head. The crop promised to be a bumper one, and he looked at it with approval.

Only a week remained until the day when he was to marry Doris. Whistling, he pushed open the gate that led into the pasture where his young heifers were grazing. He turned to shut the gate carefully behind him. At the same moment he was conscious that somebody was near him . . . someone was lurking behind a clump of briars by the pond a few yards to his left. He walked towards the spot, swinging the heavy stick which he carried.

"Here you! Come on out of that!"

Silence. Not a movement or sound in answer to his challenge.

"I'll soon have you out." Henry peered into the hiding-place. Joe Langley, pressed close to the earth, glared up at him half resentful, half afraid.

Henry shot out his arm and dragged him to his feet by his coat collar. "You little rat . . . what are you skulking here for? Didn't I tell you to clear out and keep out?" He looked with contempt at the miserable specimen before him. "Didn't I? Answer me."

Still Joe remained silent, staring at his captor. How he hated his strong, broad-shouldered figure . . . his swagger . . . the unconscious arrogance that Henry felt in his strength.

"I warned you once," Henry went on, "and that should have been sufficient." His right leg in its heavy boot shot out and caught the boy squarely on the back of his thigh. "Now get out and don't let me find you on my land again."

Joe winced a little, but refused to move. Henry laughed mockingly. "Well—what do you want?"

"You stole my girl."

"Stole your girl, did I? Say that again and I'll knock your teeth down your scrawny neck."

"You stole my girl." There was panic in Joe's whispered defiance.

Henry slapped the boy's face with the open palm of his hand, with a sound like the crack of a whip, and a flush stained the pallor of the half-wit's skin.

"Stole your girl! You haven't got a girl and never will have. You . . . looney!"

He turned on his heel and strode away. Joe stood where he was, watching the sturdy tweed-clad figure receding in the distance. Tears of fury smarted in his eyes; tears of which he felt mortified, for they were no fit accompaniment for the rage and hatred that were burning him.

Henry felt ashamed of his loss of temper. After all, the little runt wasn't quite right in the head, and perhaps he shouldn't have hit him. Uneasily he decided to tell Doris nothing of the incident. He swung along, searching the well-ordered fields for any signs of neglect.

"You'll never have a girl, you . . . looney!" The taunt rang in Joe's ears. It wasn't true. It wasn't true. The filthy swine . . . he'd been lying. Doris *was* his girl. Blindly he climbed the fence that divided Henry's land from George Isham's, and stumbled back towards his cottage.

"Is there anything you want from the village, mother? I'm meeting Henry at six and staying to supper at the farm; but I can call on my way."

"Nothing, thank you, dear. Will you be late?"

"About ten, I should think. Henry will drive me back."

"Very well. Good-bye, my dear, and enjoy yourself." Mrs. Carson kissed her daughter, and watched her hurrying down the street. Three more days and she would lose her. She felt a sentimental lump rise in her throat, and sternly told herself not to be an old fool. Doris was marrying a rich and steady man, and one who would make a good husband. "Tho' no man could wish for a better or prettier wife than my Doris," she added loyally.

Half-way to the farm the girl met Henry. At the sight of her his eyes lit up. Doris felt a warm glow of pleasure. She realised she looked her best in her new dress of flowered silk.

"Do I look nice?" she inquired a little archly. In answer Henry caught her to him, straining her body to his.

"Oh, Henry! Not here! Behave yourself!"

"I can't, Dot . . . you look so beautiful."

They went on their way in companionable silence. As they neared the house, Doris said, "Let's go for a walk before supper. It's such a lovely evening, and we've heaps of time."

"Where would you like to go?"

"The quarry?"

Henry hesitated and pulled out his watch. "It's rather a long way.... Still, we've got nearly an hour and a half." He snapped the case shut, and thrust it back into his pocket.

Too late Doris remembered her new finery and her thin shoes. "Perhaps it is rather far," she faltered.

"Nonsense. We'll do it in half an hour easily."

The sun had lost its heat and the summer evening was pleasantly cool. Ten minutes' walking brought them to a stile whence a footpath ran to the stone quarry, from which a dark green granite had been obtained that had been, in the past, much favoured by local builders. Its jagged and sombre face was brightened by wildflowers and grasses bewitching in their fresh greenery, while brambles luxuriated in pleasing disarray. Moss and short sweet grass carpeted the floor of the earlier workings, long since abandoned. And on this sun-washed evening the quarry was a lovely place—a rugged pit of lights and shadows, where bees made their music and birds throbbed their inconsequent chorus. Far above, creepers softened the outline of the rim, and fell in delicate tracery down the rough hewn stone. They came to a patch of grass, more vivid perhaps than the rest of the carpet. She sat down, carefully arranging her dress so as not to crumple it. Henry flung himself on the ground beside her.

"It's very beautiful, isn't it?" she said.

"Pretty enough! Pleased you came?"

"Yes." Her feet ached a little, and she was grateful for the rest.

His arm crept round her, drawing her to him. They lay, their heads pillowed on the grass, staring up into the sky, into the blue distance that the evening was turning to grey.

"Are you happy?"

"Yes, Henry."

He raised himself on one elbow and gazed down into her face. Slowly his head bent until his mouth was on hers. Through half-closed eyes she saw the sky through the thickness of his dark hair; felt his hands moving over her.

"Dot, my sweetest! I love you, darling ... and you're mine now." He held her very tightly, crushing her in his strong arms.

As the time for Doris's marriage drew near, Joe became more and more restless. He took to watching the little house in Marling

Lane, hoping to catch a glimpse of her. Since his last encounter with Henry he had thought it wiser to keep out of the young farmer's sight; but he frequently trailed him when he was certain that he could do so unobserved. Even his mother, drink-sodden slattern that she was, noticed his uneasiness, and chided him irritably for his "moping and carrying on," saying that his "long face fair turned her stummick, so it did."

Joe had trailed Doris at a discreet distance as she went to meet Henry, intending, if he got the opportunity and at a safe distance from the village, to plead with her once more upon the question of her coming wedding; but once Henry was her escort he abandoned the idea, deciding instead, with jealous curiosity, to spy upon them and see where they went. After a while it became obvious to him that they were making for the old granite quarry, some two miles beyond the farm, and this gave the boy an idea. Should they decide to linger awhile in the quarry itself, he could climb to the lip, approaching his objective from the other side, and so observe, without fear of discovery, what might occur. Accordingly, panting slightly from his climb, he crawled to the edge of the cutting and peered over. Almost immediately below him he saw Doris. She lay in Henry's arms, the sunlight gilding her hair. She appeared to Joe very desirable. He looked from her to Henry, and somewhere in his head a hammer seemed to beat the words, "He stole my girl. He stole my girl." Unable to tear his glance away he watched them in impotent resentment. Doris was stirring; she was pushing Henry from her. Through the still air he heard her say, "We should be getting back or we'll be late," and Henry answered, "There's no hurry, Dot." But Doris stood up, brushing tiny fragments of grass from her skirt, moving away a few paces as she did so. Henry was still lying on his back, his arms crossed behind his head. Through narrowed eyes Joe stared at him with loathing. He hated Henry's assurance. From his point of vantage he looked at his rival, envying his sleek, well-developed body. The slanting rays of the sun caught the polish on Henry's neat, highly-polished leggings, buckled round the swelling calves of his legs; glinted on the thick gold watch-chain that stretched across his stomach, already, in spite of his active life, slightly curving, with a strong threat of future corpulence.

Doris had walked away a little distance. "I want to go back," she said. "Please come, darling."

They were leaving. Joe was panic stricken.

"All right, one minute." Henry was savouring his indolence. Lazily he lit a cigarette.

Joe thought rapidly. If Henry were dead—then Doris would be his—there would be no further obstacle. But what chance had he, with his pitiful frame, against that bull of a man? He looked about him for a weapon of some kind. Only tussocks of grass grew in the scanty soil littered with a few scattered boulders far too heavy for him to lift. He must hurry; a minute more and it would be too late.

Henry was stretching in preparation to rising to his feet; a little way to his left and directly above him was an enormous rock, man high, balanced near the edge of the quarry. Joe eyed it with longing. If he could only move it! "He stole my girl," he muttered. He crossed to the stone and tested its strength, but it appeared to be embedded in the earth.

"Oh, come *on*, Henry," Doris's voice floated up to him.

Joe put his thin shoulder to the rock and pushed with all his force. It moved slightly, tottered on the brink, and disappeared over the edge. At the same instant Joe felt an agonising twinge of pain in his right ankle, and his leg gave way beneath him, bringing him down on the very rim of the pit. He felt a wave of nausea, for he had always had a horror of heights. He thought that he was falling . . . his hands clawed the air, but by some miracle he saved himself. He hung half over the chasm watching the progress of his missile. Some ten feet below the edge a thorn-bush grew precariously, springing with tenacity from a narrow ledge; and this received the full force of the rock which it caused to jump several feet outwards and to the right before the final sickening plunge of sixty feet to the ground below. As it crashed Henry had just stood up. Doris at the same instant saw what was happening. She screamed a warning and turned to run. Very suddenly her scream stopped, cut off by a dull thud. There was silence, then a man's hoarse anguished cry, "Doris. My God!"

From high above the quarry came a piteous wail, falsetto and eerie in the quiet of the evening. Henry looked up and saw the imbecile boy, flattened to the ground; heard once again the throbbing cry. He ran towards the rock and tried to move it, but even his great strength was powerless. He pushed at the huge stone, his muscles knotting with the strain, his hands raw and bleeding in his frantic efforts; until at last he realised that even if he were successful there was nothing further that he or any power could do for Doris, lying crushed beneath that appalling weight.

Grimly he ran for the mouth of the granite pit to a point where he could climb to the summit. Joe lay hugging the turf. Desperately he tried to stand, but his injured leg would not bear his weight. Wide-eyed he waited and listened. Henry was out of sight, but in a very little while he would be at the top. . . . Joe started to shriek, as a hare caught in a trap shrieks at the approach of death. He heard the thudding of heavy footsteps on earth, the laboured breathing, and Henry was upon him. He felt himself seized by a strong hand and jerked to his feet. A red-hot spasm shot through his leg. He found himself looking at a broad expanse of tweed waistcoat. Then he was lifted into the air. Seventy feet beneath him swayed the granite of the quarry floor. It seemed that he dangled over the abyss for æons. A moment of stark terror, and, released by the arm that held him, he fell. A final tortured whimper as he felt the grip relax. Then his feet scrabbled on a narrow ledge of loose chippings, a shallow scar on the rock, and his hands shot out and grasped a clump of bracken that overhung the ledge. He glanced up, and against the sky saw Henry towering immense, omnipotent. He tried to beg for mercy, but horrible sounds without meaning croaked from his throat. The bracken was snapping, frond by frond. He swayed back into space. Desperately his grime-etched hand shot out for a hold. His finger-tips touched the smooth hard leather of the farmer's gaiters, but finding no hold clutched wildly at the air. He saw the leg in front of him recede, saw a massive boot drawn back, and hesitate a moment. Then it came forward and crashed into his face. A taste of blood was in his mouth and the sharp bitterness of broken teeth. The sky reeled drunkenly and he fell, spinning, to the rocks below, where he lay as if crucified, motionless upon the stones and grass; and only the low murmur of the bees filled the pit of beauty with a drowsy peace.

THE HAPPY DANCERS

A beam of pale gold light cut the blue, smoke-dimmed atmosphere of the *Kasbek*: a beam that was focused on the arched door set under the staircase through which the artistes of the cabaret made their entrance. The lights had been lowered, and from time to time a face was thrown into momentary prominence, as its owner drew at a cigar or cigarette. All eyes were turned expectantly towards the spot where Nikakova would appear. There was a rattle of drums; the orchestra struck up a wild tzigane melody, and suddenly Nikakova was before her audience, her gaily-coloured skirts whirling around her as she twisted and spun, the vivid ribbons that hung from her tambourine dancing in grotesque rhythm.

Serge sat alone at his table, his eyes following every movement of the dancer before him; and as he watched the way in which she captured her audience, and as he joined in the salvo of applause that greeted the end of her performance, he remembered his first meeting with her three, no four, years previously.

He had seen her as he was riding through the village at Zaramow—very proud and brave in his new uniform—and on his first leave from the military school in Petrograd. She was barely seventeen, and he some four years her senior. She was dancing, then, to a group of peasants; and he had been struck by her grace, and amazed that the village could have produced a daughter so delicately beautiful. He was used to the massive and comely buxomness of the country women; but this slender elfin charm, fragile as porcelain . . .

And silently he had waited on his horse until she had looked up and caught his intent gaze. And then she had become confused and stopped abruptly, and her audience had looked up and seen the cause of her discomfiture, and an embarrassed hush had descended abruptly on the laughing group.

He had beckoned to her to come to him, and had asked her name. She told him that she was Louba Kerensky, the daughter of Boris Kerensky; and Serge had frowned with displeasure, for her father was a man whose ideas were radical in the extreme—a surly drunken brute, always ready to stir up discontent and trouble. Serge's father, the Grand Duke, had had him beaten some months before, and had threatened him with Siberia should further correction be necessary.

Serge found it incredible that this frail girl could be his daughter. He smiled down at her. "You dance divinely—where did you learn?"

Louba smiled. "Learn? Where should *I* have dancing lessons? I learned from the wind in the trees, and the streams dancing over their pebbled beds, and from the sun dancing on the surface of the lake; and from the butterflies dancing over the coloured flowers, and"—she glanced up at him—"from the laughter dancing in my Lord's eyes." And she threw back her head and laughed up at him, vital in her gypsy beauty.

Serge was interested. She was clever, this girl—as well as attractive. He tapped his riding-boot with his cane.

"The best of schools, my dear ... but are all your teachers, then, so gay?"

"No. ... I learned also from the corpses dancing on the gallows, and the flies dancing on the dungheaps, and from Death dancing near starving men during the hard winters of my childhood."

"A thorough education!"

Serge was intrigued. Well, he was home for six weeks, and a little diversion would help to bring nearer his return to Petrograd and the new friends he had made there.

But when the time had come, he had taken Louba with him —to have her trained as a dancer; and also because he could not give her up.

He noticed with surprise that his cigar had gone out, and as he struck a match he saw Louba threading her way through the tables towards him, eyes bright with the pleasure of success, lips parted in a smile as she received compliments from the officers and their friends seated in parties round the great semi-circle of the dance floor. Teeth flushed white under dark moustaches as heads turned to follow her.

And as she came, Louba too remembered her first meeting with Serge, how, from the depths that separated them, she had always admired him, and how she had been determined to make the most of her opportunity; and then how she had come to love him sincerely. When Serge had first taken her, Boris had threatened to kill him, had raved of the injustice of a world where the aristocrats ground down the peasants, bleeding them of their money, battening on their labours, raping their daughters. But the more level-headed of the villagers had restrained him from taking any such action that could only end in failure and disgrace, and that would mean for Boris the salt mines of Siberia.

Louba had never seen her father these last four years, and he, she knew, had no knowledge of where she was, or of the high position she had gained for herself by her talent and with her lover's help. Boris had loved her in a fierce incoherent way, with a passionate almost frightening love . . . but she was finished with the peasant life—thank God—with the filth and the squalor and the clumsy-handed oafs. She had Serge, admiration, money, comfort and success; and life was indeed good.

Louba rested her hand lightly on Serge's shoulder as she sank on to the chair by his side.

"You liked my performance to-night?"

"Magnificent as always, my darling. And your audience—they loved you."

"If I danced well it was for you—only for you. You still believe that?"

"And when I'm not here?"

"Your table is always empty. I will not allow others to occupy it!"

Serge's adoring smile was her answer. He poured her out a glass of champagne.

"You look a little tired, my sweet. Drink this, it will do you good."

"You know I never drink. When I dance I cannot drink."

"I know, Louba. But you do not dance again to-night. Drink with me—to our future happiness." She raised her glass, her exquisite brown eyes smiling into his, blue and steady.

"To our future happiness!"

But in his heart Serge was ill at ease. Who knew what was going to happen in the future? Even a day from that moment—to-morrow his leave was up, and he went back to the war.

It was the early spring of 1917.

As they were leaving the club, Louba paused in front of the great golden doorway and gazed up at the sky; she wore an evening coat of white satin, with a huge fur collar, that emphasised the delicacy of her slender neck.

"How lovely the night is—but Serge, so short ... and to-morrow you return ... to what?" Her beauty was startling, etched against the background of the night.

Serge beckoned to a commissionaire, and in a few seconds the long low motor car that he had given Louba slid silently to the kerb. He looked at the clock. It was nearly three o'clock. The night air was cool and very sweet.

"Louba, my darling, in five hours I shall be gone."

Her hand clutched his convulsively. There was silence, each questioning what the future held for them. Then Louba spoke, her voice trying to disguise the fear that filled her mind. She would not talk of the morrow.

"Tretkoff told me that he was going to change the name of the *Kasbek* to *The Happy Dancers*."

"Why?"

"Because it's the one oasis of real gaiety in this war-shadowed city."

"And when will this momentous change occur?"

"After he's completed the redecorations. It's to be closed next week for that reason. On your next leave you'll hardly recognise it!"

His next leave ... when would that be?

The car stopped outside Louba's house. Serge turned to the chauffeur.

"Be here at half-past seven."

They walked slowly up the steps; and the sky grew lighter as the hours passed and the faery fingers of the dawn trailed their ragged banners over Petrograd.

*

Some months later Louba sat in front of the triple mirror on her dressing-table. It would soon be time for her to start for *The Happy Dancers*, where she was to dance for the last time. She frowned as she rubbed a little rouge into her flawless skin. She was frightened; frightened of Petrograd and the feeling of unrest and hatred that permeated the city.

And Boris was there, she knew; she had read that he had been one of the agitators who had been arrested that morning and later released. She prayed that he wouldn't discover where she was; but reassured herself that there was little chance of that, for she had changed her name, and there was small likelihood of his connecting his daughter Louba with Nikakova the famous caba-ret dancer. Yes—she was dancing to-night for the last time. She was excited and happy, oh so happy. For Serge. When would he come back? She couldn't tell him in a letter. Serge's child! Her mouth was very tender. She peered once more into her looking-glass, tracing the chiselled lines of her lips with crimson. She could see the room behind her reflected in the mirror; the thick rose carpet, the lights, the broad low bed, and the door. Her eyes widened, her hand was motionless, still clutching her lipstick, for the door was quietly opening. Gently, an inch at a time. Now she could see a man's arm, and the toe of a highly-polished riding-boot. And then he was in the room, and a cry of joy rang out.

"Serge!" He was at her side in three strides, and she was in his arms, his mouth pressed on hers, hard and insistent.

"Darling!"

"But why didn't you let me know you were coming?" She pushed him gently away. "Let me look at you." She put up her left hand and stroked his hair. "Serge . . . for how long?"

"Twenty-four hours. I only knew myself six hours ago. Every-thing has been so unsettled. Rumours everywhere. And on the way from the station there were angry crowds. Louba, I don't like your being here in Petrograd. To-morrow you must leave. It's not safe."

"I'm all right, my dear. But come, I must go to the Club. I dance there to-night—my swan song!"

And in the privacy of the motor car while they made their slow way through the crowd-blocked streets, she told him of their coming child. The journey was slow, and several times their way was blocked. Angry voices shouted at them, and once a stone hit the shining bonnet.

"Serge! My father is here."

"I know, darling. I saw him in the street on my way to your house. He was addressing a crowd of people outside the Nicholas Theatre."

"And he saw you?"

"Yes . . . I don't know . . . what does it matter?" He pressed her hand reassuringly.

"Oh, but it does! What will he do? . . . He means you harm. The city has gone mad. I'm frightened."

"It's nothing, darling. What *can* he do, here, in Petrograd?"

"But you haven't been here the last few days. There has been rioting; and shops have been looted and smashed. The police seem quite incapable of doing anything to stop it."

"Or perhaps they don't want to."

"What do you mean?" Louba whispered.

Serge shrugged his shoulders, and drawing her to him kissed her very gently.

The Happy Dancers was full. But there was a breathless frenzied quality in the gaiety that was new. And two military policemen stood by the gilded doorway. As they went in one of them saluted, and said to Serge:

"I shouldn't go there to-night, there might be trouble."

Louba overheard his warning, and said, "But we must; I dance here."

The incident had left a fear in the back of her mind that increased as the evening wore on. Distant shouting was heard, and once the brittle rattle of rifle-fire. A sudden silence descended on the diners, but only for a moment. As if to combat this vague menace, a hectic babble of talk and laughter broke out. But the laughter was forced and more drinks were called for. Tretkoff spoke to the leader of the orchestra. The music must be louder and with no intervals of silence.

Boris Kerensky was drunk. His ragged beard was matted with the thick dark beer that had evaded his mouth. He peered at his companions, men and women sunk as low as himself, and all in varying stages of intoxication.

"And you say you know where Serge Poliakoff is?" he repeated, peering into the face of his companion.

"Yes. My brother is the bastard's chauffeur. You'd find him at *The Happy Dancers*—that's where his tart dances," replied the man. "They'll be dancing to a different tune soon," he went on, "the bloody swine." He spat on the floor in his disgust.

Boris got uncertainly to his feet, his brain occupied with one idea. Revenge. Revenge on Serge for taking Louba—his adorable Louba. It should be easy to-night. His foot slithered in a pool of spittle. He laughed. It had been hard to wait, but now the time had come. He clambered unsteadily on to the rough wooden table and started to harangue the clients of the squalid drinking house.

Tretkoff made a sign to the band and walked into the middle of the dancing floor. The babble of talk died down, and an expectant hush fell as they waited for him to speak. Louba had just finished her dance and had rejoined Serge.

"Ladies and gentlemen," the night-club proprietor announced, "the club will now be closed for the night. I have received information that it would be wiser for you all to go to your homes. Thank you."

He turned and walked off the floor.

Immediately a stir ruffled the tables. Women struggled into their coats, collected their scattered hand-bags. Men called loudly for their bills. Serge and Louba watched the confusion.

"Shall we go, darling?" Serge suggested.

"In a few minutes," she answered. "I want to have a short talk with Tretkoff and collect my things from my dressing-room. Wait until the others have gone."

In fifteen minutes the restaurant was empty, save for a few sullen waiters whisking away the dirty plates and glasses. Serge saw the little proprietor looking at him. He raised his hand.

"What's the trouble?" he asked, when Tretkoff stood beside him. "Is it serious . . . or just a scare?"

"Who knows? The crowds are out of hand, and in an ugly

mood. There has been skirmishing in many parts of the city. I am now shutting up as quickly as I can. I don't want any trouble here."

One by one the lights were extinguished.

"You go up, Serge," Louba said. "I'll join you in a few minutes. Get the car."

Serge walked up the staircase. The club had quite a different atmosphere when it was empty. Depressing and tawdry. The big doors into the street were shut. He rapped on them impatiently with his cane. A small door set at the side was opened by a porter, who came out of his alcove on the right.

"Mlle. Nikakova is coming in a few minutes."

It was very cold in the open air, and over the roofs Serge saw a red glow, as if a building was ablaze. His car was nowhere to be seen. He heard shouts in an alley near at hand. He wondered how long Louba would be. The shouting was nearer now; a figure ran into the end of the street where Serge stood, handsome in his uniform, against the painted gold of the wooden door. Three or four men followed the first, and then more came until the street was filled. They surged towards him, singing and laughing. Several of the men were carrying bottles; others had rifles and swords.

"Hey! there's one of the bloody officers!" a woman shouted. Her cry directed the attention of the whole band to Serge. In a moment he was surrounded by a jeering menacing mob, drunken and bestial, lusting for cruelty. Serge looked at them. He must not show his fear. Among the brutal faces he saw one he knew. Boris Kerensky. Their eyes met, and Serge read the light of insane rage and triumph in those of his opponent. He bellowed for silence and started haranguing the crowd, telling of the Grand Duke's treatment of his peasants; of Serge's violation of Louba, his daughter. He called upon them to take the law into their own hands, to make Serge suffer, as he and his had made the people suffer. The attitude of the crowd was threatening, they closed round wolfishly. Then Kerensky stepped forward, his face contorted into a mask of rage, and spat in Serge's face.

For a moment Serge stood still, the next, his arm flew out; and Boris lay stretched on the pavement.

And then Serge was overwhelmed. As he went down he saw

the door open, caught a glimpse of Louba's horrified face, cried "Go back!" saw a giant soldier seize her. He struggled towards her, but a terrific blow with a rifle-butt caught him on the side of the head. He fell as if pole-axed.

Five minutes later he opened his eyes. His head felt as if it was splitting. He groaned ... vague noises sounded in his ears. A brutal kick roused him. He was roughly pulled to his feet. Nothing seemed real. He was not fully conscious. Somewhere he heard a woman screaming; then roars of laughter and coarse mocking shouts. He wondered who the woman was and why she was screaming. And then he realised it was Louba. He staggered towards her, but was held back by muscular arms. His own were tightly tied behind his back. The stench of the men who were holding him was overpowering. The cord hurt—cutting into the flesh of his wrists. What had happened? What was Louba saying? He couldn't hear. . . . Yes, it was clearer now . . .

" . . . You can't do it to me . . . I'm one of you . . . dear Lord . . . I swear it. Help . . . help . . ." Her voice rose to a scream. "Serge . . ." He strained to get to her, his chest heaving with the exertion; but the men who held him were strong. And now they were forcing her against the door—the golden door. God! what were they doing? Those great nails . . . the hammer. . . .

When Boris Kerensky recovered consciousness the street was deserted. He lay huddled in the gutter, his eyes half closed. Dimly he heard shouts, the clatter of horses' hoofs, the rattle of gunfire, cheers and groans. The sky was red with the blaze of burning buildings. He turned his head. To his right stood the golden door of *The Happy Dancers*, and nailed to it, crucified, hung Serge Polia-koff; his stripped body white against the gilt, very white, relieved only by the crimson stigmata. He was dead. By his side hung the naked body of a girl, her flesh rent by a vicious sword thrust. As he looked, her eyelids fluttered faintly, and she slowly opened her eyes, glazing with the film of death.

Boris looked once more into the eyes of Louba.

THE ACTOR'S STORY

"I'm afraid I have never had any personal experience of ghosts," the speaker apologised, "so that I can't cap your stories with one of my own, but I was once a witness of a particularly unpleasant happening."

David Lang leant against the mantelpiece, his hands thrust deep into his pockets. It was eleven o'clock at night, and the six men present, mellowed after their port and cigars, sat in a semi-circle of large leather armchairs round the blazing fire. I had asked if I might bring David to our monthly gathering at which the members of our little "club" took it in turn to relate some psychic adventure or weird occurrence. Old Norman Strathers had just finished an account of an elemental that had recently caused a good deal of trouble to a friend of his in Cornwall; and, as his narrative had been short, and it was still early, David had been called upon to give us "a bed-time story."

His audience settled down in greater comfort to listen. Pipes were filled and lit; and the pleasant splash of soda-water splutter-ing into whisky-glasses increased the atmosphere of interested attention. David threw away the stub of his cigar, and sat on the arm of my chair.

"As you may know," he began, "by profession I am an actor. Well; about three years ago I was with Margaret Carter on tour. We were playing the bigger towns in the Midlands, and included in our repertoire was a programme of Grand Guignol plays. We were quite a small company: Margaret, her husband, John Fieldon, Mark Hastings, myself, Philippa Burton, and three or four small-part people. On the whole the tour had been a success-ful one, and I think that we had all enjoyed it. Margaret is charm-ing to work with, and I might say that we were all very good friends without any of the usual professional jealousies and spites that are unfortunately so often found among my fellow artists.

The only discordant note was Philippa Burton. She was a very fine actress, but decidedly temperamental, and was head over heels in love with Hastings. Apparently he returned her feelings; for they were seldom apart, and the rest of us were waiting to hear that they were engaged to be married. Philippa was perfectly beautiful in a dark Spanish way, and could, when she chose, be one of the most charming and amusing women that I have ever met. But she was insanely jealous, and made the most fantastic scenes if she thought Hastings paid any attention to anyone but herself. I think, in a way, that he was rather flattered by this, and enjoyed the feeling of power over her that it gave him. At the beginning, these scenes were comparatively infrequent, but as the weeks went on they became more and more regular until the work of both of them began to suffer in consequence. There was a strong feeling of constraint, and we all felt that it would be a very good thing for all concerned when the tour finished.

I don't want to give the impression that Philippa was a jealous shrew. She wasn't, by any means, and Hastings treated her very badly. He was a strikingly handsome man, utterly selfish and self-indulgent; and perhaps it was only natural that he responded to the advances made to him by women. About this time there was a girl in the company—Nora Cummings—a pretty but rather ordinary little blonde who had set her cap at him, and who was obviously much pleased by his response. To a woman of Philippa's talent and nature such competition must have been galling in the extreme . . . but I'm getting away from the story.

Our last date was a week in Lacington—at a small theatre of an intimate character, and Margaret had decided to give a play of Ibsen's for the major part of the week, and the Grand Guignol plays on the Saturday night and matinée. We were all feeling sorry that the tour was ending, yet glad to be going back to London; and what with making our own plans for the immediate future, and the inevitable flurry of the last days, we had given less of our attention to Philippa and Hastings than we should otherwise have done.

Ibsen's play had done surprisingly good business, and the company was in a very cheerful frame of mind; but Margaret's part in the play was a long and difficult one, and we were glad to finish up with the laughs and melodrama of our "horrors." We were giving five plays; two short farces and three blood curdlers. One of the latter was a delightful little piece about a nurse who picked out the eyes of her ex-lover when he was lying strapped on an operating table. It had only four characters; played by Philippa, Hastings—the unfortunate victim—Fieldon, and myself; and it was one of the two big thrills of the evening.

Well, the matinée played to a packed house, and we were much gratified by the gasps and screams from the auditorium. After the performance, since there was only two hours to wait before getting ready for the night's show, I went to Margaret's dressing-room to have a drink and talk over the previous week's happenings, as was my usual custom. As it happened, Fieldon was not there on that evening, and Margaret and I were alone. We talked about our success at the matinée and our sorrow that the tour was over; and then suddenly, she said:

"David—did you notice anything odd about Philippa this afternoon?"

I answered that she had appeared nervous and depressed, but that I had become accustomed to that, and that Hastings had certainly done enough to annoy her by his behaviour with Nora Cummings.

"Yes, I know," Margaret continued, "but she looked different to-day somehow—more as if she was . . . desperate. It's difficult to explain, but she . . . frightened me."

I told her that as it was our last night everything would be all right, and that Philippa and Hastings would be less on each other's nerves once they got back to London; and that there was no need for Margaret to feel responsible for, in any case, they were a grown man and woman and should be perfectly capable of looking after their own affairs. Margaret didn't seem greatly reassured by this answer, and we talked of other things until about seven, when it was time for me to go and make up, and get into the peasant clothes in which I made my first appearance.

I had just determined to go when there was a knock on the door. Margaret raised her eyebrows in inquiry. I shrugged my shoulders. Then she called out, "Come in," and the door opened and Hastings stood there holding Nora Cummings by the hand. They were both smiling and looking extremely embarrassed. I glanced at Margaret.

"Oh, Miss Carter," Nora spoke quickly and breathlessly, "Mark and I thought . . . we wanted to tell you . . . I mean . . ." she trailed off in confusion.

"Yes?" Margaret smiled at the girl.

"We wanted to tell you we're married," Hastings broke in, his deep voice husky with happiness.

Margaret, in spite of the shock, acted magnificently. She crossed over to Nora and kissed her.

"My dear, I'm so glad. I know you'll be very happy," she turned to Mark. "And you're a very lucky man—but I can see you know that already!"

For a moment I was too stunned to say anything—but the thought crossed my mind . . . "Does Philippa know?" I wondered if Mark had told her. If so, God knows what her performance would be like that night.

"And now," Margaret said, "you must both go and get ready— or we'll be late starting. We'll have a celebration after the show."

"We wanted to tell you first," Hastings said.

"Yes—you're the first to know," Nora added.

They turned away, Mark's great shoulders almost filling the narrow doorway, his head bent as he smiled down at the girl beside him.

When they had gone there was a short silence—then Margaret and I spoke simultaneously, and we both said the same thing.

"We must tell Philippa—she mustn't hear from Nora."

"Will you tell her?" I asked.

"Yes—ask her to come here, will you?"

On my way to my dressing-room I knocked on her door. She had just come to the theatre and hadn't started to change. She didn't appear until the middle of the second play, and therefore had three-quarters of an hour longer than Margaret or I. "Oh, Philippa," I said, "Margaret wants you for a minute."

She looked rather surprised; and I hurried to my own room, wishing to God that it was all over, and feeling as sorry as hell for the poor woman. When I was ready I looked at my watch that was lying on the dressing-table. It pointed to twenty past seven. That left ten minutes before it was time for the show to begin. I decided to go and ask Margaret how Philippa had taken the news.

As I walked down the passage I saw her going into her room. She was in her street clothes, and had evidently been out again since I had last seen her. I knocked on Margaret's door. She was sitting at her dressing-table—smearing make-up on her face.

"Well?" I asked.

"I'll tell you about it after the first play. I'm terribly late. It was awful, David. She seemed stunned—as if something in her had died. Go now—or I'll never be ready."

I went on to the stage and peered through a hole in the curtain at the "House." It was filling up rapidly; and a low buzz of conversation came from the auditorium.

I thought how odd it was that the audience should sit there waiting to see our plays, and little knowing the real dramas that were going on back stage at this moment.

"Programme ... choc-o-lates," the girl's voice rose above the hum of talk as she walked up the centre gangway.

The orchestra began its first number.

"Mr. Lang!"

I started as I heard Nora Cummings' voice at my elbow; I stepped back, and knocked over a property rake that leant against the "farm-house" wall. It fell to the floor with a clatter. Nora was already dressed and made up, her blonde hair covered by a bandanna handkerchief.

"Mr. Lang!" she repeated, "I don't know *what* Miss Burton will say—do *you*?" she giggled anxiously.

And now other people were coming on to the stage, and the big lights from the sides were switched on. I heard the call-boy shouting, "Beginners on to the stage, please." Then—"Clear the stage!" The orchestra worked itself into a final frenzy; the lights in the auditorium dimmed—and the play began.

I don't think that either Margaret or myself excelled ourselves, and as soon as it was over I hurried to her room. She repeated what she had told me before, and then added, "I can't believe that Mark could have done such a thing. Why, David, the man must be a fiend! Poor, poor Philippa!"

But Philippa's control was perfect. In her first play she gave a wonderful performance, and vanished directly afterwards into her dressing-room and locked the door. I didn't see her again until just before the final play—*Suspicion*; when I stood beside her in the wings waiting for our entrance. She was very pale, and a little muscle at the corner of her mouth was twitching, but otherwise she gave no sign of the shock she had received.

Now this last playlet was in two scenes—a private ward, and an operating theatre; and it was in the second scene that Philippa did her eye-picking act. She was alone on the stage with Hastings, and did her "stuff" with her back to the audience—Mark's screams of agony being the final curtain.

The play had gone very well so far, and I stood watching the last moments, together with the other members of the cast, waiting to troup on to the stage for the applause and, as it was the Saturday night, Margaret's speech of thanks.

There was a short wait of a little more than a minute between the two scenes, and I was struck by Philippa's appearance. She was leaning against a side pillar, her eyes closed, the long lashes thickly black against the pallor of her skin. Her face bore an expression of such sorrow as I have never seen before or since. Then she opened her eyes, and they blazed with an anger that I pray I may never see again. She caught my glance and smiled. I asked her if she was feeling all right, and she said, "Yes," and turned away. I thought I'd speak to Margaret about her before she went on, but there wasn't time, for the scene was ready and the curtain went up. I saw Margaret standing in the wings opposite, so I went behind the scenes to join her. On my way, I met Fieldon, who talked to me about the plans for the following day, and by the time I eventually reached Margaret, Philippa was in the middle of her tirade of hate and revenge to the bound Hastings, in which she accused him of being faithless, and as she leant over him to smear the "blood" round his eyeballs I noticed that she had forgotten the bottle she usually held containing the necessary colourful liquid. I remember faintly regretting that the audience would be deprived of its final thrill.

And now she was bending over Mark's face and he was screaming. God, how he screamed! The audience sat spellbound while the hideous shrieks filled the theatre; terrible hoarse cries that made even the company shudder. And then Hastings did something that was not in the script. He broke the workmanlike "prop" straps that tied him to the table, and staggered towards Philippa, shouting, "My eyes ... my eyes ... God ..." but he missed her and groped towards the footlights, screaming and mouthing at the audience; his hands clawing at the empty air. I glanced at Margaret beside me, and her face was set in a mask of horror. She made a sign to the man who worked the curtain, and it came down abruptly in the dead silence that can be the greatest tribute to acting.

And then the rattle of applause came and the curtain went up again, and Hastings was still tearing at his eyes and screaming. He flung out his hands, took a step forward, and fell into the orchestra pit.

Of course pandemonium broke loose in the audience.

David stopped and felt in his pocket for his cigarette case. Nobody spoke.

"Yes," he finished, "you were right. Philippa gave too realistic a performance."

SPECIAL DIET

"Of course I quite understand your feelings in this matter, Mrs. Willoughby, but I can't help thinking that it would be better to send your mother to a private home, where she will have every possible care. There is no chance at all of her complete recovery, and in my opinion it would be far better to put the responsibility of such a case on those whose job it is to bear it."

Mrs. Willoughby looked at the doctor with troubled eyes. "But she'd hate that! However well such homes are run, there is always the feeling of being hemmed in . . . a prisoner. It would kill my mother . . . and when she's not going through one of her phases, she's as sane as you or I."

"Well, I leave the decision in your hands. If you think that keeping her here is the best course; as long as she gets no worse, then I have no more to say. You had better get a night nurse as well as Nurse Charteris; and above all, Mrs. Hinton must not be left alone day or night. I know of a very reliable woman I can get for you. I'll send her round to see you this afternoon."

The young doctor pulled out his watch, glanced at it and continued: "If we find that such an arrangement is not satisfactory, then I am afraid that we will have to make other arrangements." As he spoke he picked up his hat and gloves from an oak chest that stood in the hall.

Mrs. Willoughby followed him down the steps to his car—a spruce Buick.

"Very well, and thank you so much for all your trouble. I know that you will do all in your power to help me. But I can't bear to think of my mother shut up in one of those places." She held out her hand. The pale sunshine of the early spring morning fell pleasantly on her honey-coloured hair.

Doctor Burleigh smiled at her with admiration. He felt sorry for this girl, still in her twenties, and left a widow the previous year, her husband having been killed in an aeroplane crash. And now this fresh trouble with her mother. He was afraid that she would have to be sent to an institution in the near future. However, as long as there was ample supervision there could be no harm in trying this other plan first.

He pressed the self-starter, turning to wave his hand as the car slid forward. Mrs. Willoughby walked slowly up the steps to the door. She was certain that she was doing the best thing. She glanced at the clock in the drawing-room. Eleven o'clock. It was time to do the marketing for the house. She wondered where Mary could be. Her school did not re-open until the following Monday, and she knew that the child enjoyed going with her to the shops. She crossed to the door that led into the garden.

"Mary! Mar-y!"

The door from the kitchen quarters opened, and the parlour-maid, carrying a tray laden with silver, paused to say: "I think Miss Mary is up with Nurse and Mrs. Hinton, madam."

Mrs. Willoughby thanked her, and ran up the staircase that led to her mother's room. Softly she opened the door. The old lady was sitting on a sofa in the sun-flooded bay window, a half-finished scarf of brilliant orange flowing from her lap. Her face was fat and of an unhealthy pallor. At her feet lay Mary, poring over a much tattered and dog-eared photograph album.

"Oh, Granny—did you *really* wear clothes like that?" she asked incredulously, pointing a grubby finger at a photograph of a woman heavily protected against the terrors of motoring in the 'nineties.

"Yes, dear child."

Mrs. Hinton looked up as her daughter came in. "You haven't come to take Mary away from me already, have you, dear?"

"It's time to do the shopping. Is there anything you want, darling?"

"No, I don't think so. Unless you can think of anything, Nurse?" she added, turning to Nurse Charteris, who sat in a chair by her side, reading the paper.

"No, Mrs. Hinton, I don't think there's anything you require this morning."

"Run and get your coat on, Mary," Mrs. Willoughby said, "and meet me in the hall. I'll be ready as soon as you are. And wash your hands," she called, after the retreating figure of her eight-year-old daughter.

Mrs. Hinton glanced up at her. Her eyes narrowed, and a cunning smile played at the corners of her mouth.

"And what did that young doctor say to you to-day? That I'm worse, eh? A mad old woman, I suppose he called me. That young man wants to shut me up. Go on—tell me."

"Don't be silly, Mother. Of course he doesn't. Doctor Burleigh's very fond of you. If you want to know, he said that you were getting on very nicely; but that you need rest and quiet and feeding up to get back your strength. He's going to order you a special diet; and we're going to have a night nurse so that Nurse Charteris will have more time to go out."

"So he's afraid to leave me alone. Is that it?" Mrs. Hinton threw her knitting angrily on to the floor. "I won't stand it, do you hear? I won't stand it. Treating me as if I were a criminal or a maniac!"

She was working herself up into a rage; her face became suffused with colour, and little flecks of foam escaped from her mouth and ran down her chin.

"Now, Mrs. Hinton, there's nothing to be excited about," soothed Nurse Charteris, giving Mrs. Willoughby a look that said: "You'd better go. I can manage her better by myself."

"You want to put me away. You're all in league against me. That's what it is!"

"No, Mother, we're not. You mustn't get ideas like that into your head. I must go now. Mary will be waiting for me."

"Mary's the only one of you that loves me at all," the old woman whimpered, rocking her heavy body backwards and forwards in an agony of self-pity. "So the doctor ordered me a special diet, eh? What's it to be? But I suppose I'm not fit to be told?"

"Of course you are, darling. He ordered you plenty of milk, soups, and very lightly cooked meat, as nearly raw as you can eat. And not too much strong tea," she finished laughingly.

"So I'm even to be deprived of my tea," Mrs. Hinton grumbled. Her daughter took this opportunity to tiptoe quietly out of the room and downstairs to where Mary waited for her: her little face aglow with health under the jaunty red beret; her long thin legs coltishly graceful in their prosaic black woollen stockings.

"Come *on*, Mummy. You have been a long time!"

Together they walked down the street to the shopping district of the town. Joan Willoughby, youthful in her simple jersey and skirt; Mary laughing and chattering beside her.

In Mrs. Hinton's room Nurse Charteris was having difficulty in calming her patient, who was, in her private opinion, a nasty spiteful old woman, and one who would be far better in a Home. No one knew her sly cruel little ways like she did. Mrs. Willoughby was a lot too soft hearted. And it wasn't right that the child should be allowed to run in and out of the old woman's room. She'd speak to the doctor about it the next time that he called. Wicked it would be, if Mrs. Hinton had one of her spasms when Mary was there!

Nurse Charteris looked with satisfaction at her well-developed body. *She* could take care of herself. But a child was different. She was glad that a night nurse was coming to help her. They should have had one long since.

Nurse Charteris sniffed.

"One more word from you, Mrs. Hinton," she snapped, "and I won't let you have an egg for your tea."

She often made use of the old woman's greed for disciplinarian purposes. She had discovered at a very early stage that this was the easiest way to control her. Mrs. Hinton shot her a venomous look: a look of hatred. Then, bending down, she picked up her knitting; and soon the only sounds that disturbed the silence of the room were the occasional rustle of Nurse Charteris turning a page of her paper and the incessant clicking of Mrs. Hinton's knitting needles.

A week had gone by since the arrival of the night nurse, a big-boned cockney of Scotch extraction, who rejoiced in the name of Flora McBride. In appearance more masculine than feminine, when off duty she dressed herself incongruously in pale pinks and blues, and told endless stories in which her friends constantly addressed her as "Flossy" or "Flo"; and in which she narrowly avoided the persistent and perilous advances of "men."

After their first meeting Mrs. Hinton appeared to have accepted her presence and, apart from being rather more silent and morose than was usual, her progress appeared to suffer no serious setback. She seemed, however, very nervous concerning her own health, and ceaselessly bombarded both Joan and the two nurses with questions about the doctor's report on her condition; and whether her new diet was proving adequate. For long periods, too, she would sit, her hands folded on her knees, staring in silence into the glowing heart of the fire, paying no attention when spoken to, but occasionally shaping words with her mouth as if she was whispering secrets to herself.

Nurse Charteris had spoken to Doctor Burleigh regarding Mary's visits to her grandmother, and the doctor had agreed that the sooner they ceased the better it would be for the child. He had explained to Joan that it would upset the old lady if Mary stopped seeing her altogether. "But," he added, "let a greater time elapse between each visit. As yet your daughter doesn't realise that your mother is, shall we say, unhinged; and she is at a very impressionable age. It would be a terrible thing if she were frightened in any way." He stood leaning against the mantelpiece, one hand thrust deep into his trousers pocket, the other playing idly with the long links of his watch-chain. "I must tell you," he continued, "that this present arrangement cannot last more than a few months. I see no sign of improvement in your mother's condition. I'm afraid that you will have to reconcile yourself to sending her away."

In the evening when Joan went to say good night to Mrs. Hinton, the old woman said: "I know what you're going to tell me. 'The doctor said he was very satisfied.' Well! I don't believe it. I want more feeding up—more meat. I'm not given enough to keep a canary alive!" She shivered. "My old bones can't stand these March winds."

A few days after this Nurse Charteris came to Joan in a state of considerable excitement. "Mrs. Willoughby, I think the time has come when you *must* make some other arrangement for your mother. I don't feel I can be responsible for her any longer. Why, I'd never have believed it of her! It makes me shudder even now, when I think of it!" She paused for breath.

"But what is it, Nurse? What's happened?"

"When we came into breakfast this morning we saw that there

was a mouse in the trap; and I thought that it could stay there until we'd finished, when I'd give it to Thompson to give to the cat. Well, would you believe it, after we'd finished I left the room for a moment to call him, and when I came back, there was Mrs. Hinton cutting the beast's head off with a table-knife. I called to her to stop, and asked what she was doing, and what do you think she replied?" Nurse Charteris paused impressively. "She replied that she wanted to drink its blood to get back her own strength. 'Disgusting,' I said. Can you *imagine* it?" She wagged her head with meaning. "I must go back now, or goodness knows what she'll be up to next."

When Joan repeated the story to Doctor Burleigh, he looked very grave. "That settles it," he said. "I'm sorry; but I have no alternative. Your mother must go to a home; and as soon as possible. I'll try to arrange for her to be received early in the week."

Joan had cried, but he had sat by her side and held her hands in his own, and had told her of other cases where the same strain of cruelty had developed, and where there had been nothing else to be done.

And so at length Joan was convinced, and all arrangements were made for Mrs. Hinton to go to the "Parkside Home for Mental Cases" on the following Tuesday. It had been decided to say nothing to the old lady; and once the decision had been reached that there was no other course to take, Joan felt as if a load had been taken off her mind.

Nurse Charteris said, "High time, too," when she heard the news; while McBride tossed her head coyly, and boomed in her deep voice: "Such goings on make a girl feel quite creepy. I never could take much to mentals."

Monday came; and suitcases and trunks spilled tissue and newspaper in the nurses' rooms, and grazed the legs of the unwary on the landing. Great care was taken that the old woman should gain no inkling of its true purpose. When she questioned the hurried comings and goings of the nurses and Joan, she was told that Nurse McBride was leaving, a statement that both satisfied and pleased her. She sat on her sofa, and watched with triumph and malignancy her awkward movements as she busied herself with the tea-table. The ambulance with its white-coated attendants was due at nine o'clock on the following day, so that there would be little time in the morning to do much.

During tea Nurse McBride, who officially did not come on duty until ten o'clock, but who had been unable to sleep during the afternoon owing to the bustle that pervaded the house, said to Nurse Charteris: "I think I'll just slip round to Boots', dear. I won't be long. I've run out of perfume."

Nurse Charteris looked at her colleague in surprise. She was always bewildered by this gaunt woman's coquettish airs.

"If it wouldn't be a trouble would you get me a bottle of aspirin?"

"Certainly, dear." Nurse McBride got up. "Well, I think I'll run along now. Ta-ta!" She hurried from the room.

Mrs. Hinton's voice broke the silence. It had that harsh imper-sonal sound that is so often found among deaf persons.

"Thank God that terrible woman is going tomorrow. She's as common as dirt, and a conceited fool into the bargain."

Nurse Charteris smiled a little grimly. Although she shared the opinion of her patient, she thought it a wiser policy to say nothing. She was spared the necessity of answering, for at that moment the door opened and Thompson, the butler, entered. He crossed to Nurse Charteris.

"If you please, Nurse, you are wanted on the telephone."

"Who is it?"

"I didn't catch the name." He knew perfectly well that it was the doctor's voice, but had been warned not to mention his name in front of "the old looney."

"Please say I'm just coming."

He went out, and left the two women alone. Mrs. Hinton gave her a glance of suspicious inquiry.

"I won't be long, my dear," said Nurse Charteris; and she bus-tled down the stairs after Thompson, wondering who it could be.

Left by herself Mrs. Hinton wandered to the window; and as she looked into the drive she saw Mary dashing up it on her bicycle. She knocked on the glass, trying to attract her attention. She was too far off for the little girl to hear, but at that instant she happened to look up and saw her grandmother smiling at her and beckoning to her to come up. "Poor old thing," she reflected, "stuck up there in her room all the time." The child nodded her head in assent and ran into the house.

Mrs. Hinton smiled to herself; Nurse would be away longer than she had said—the interfering chatterbox!

A minute more and she heard light steps running along the passage.

"Granny!" Mary called through the half-opened door.

"Hush, child! Don't make so much noise. I've got rather a headache—but come in, my dear, come in!" Mary ran to the sofa and held up her face to be kissed. She thought her grandmother looked strange; her eyes were fixed on her face; on her throat . . . with an odd expression of . . . Mary tried to describe it—of almost hungry yearning.

"Sit here, child. I haven't got much time. They never will leave me alone. But I want to talk to you. I'm an ill old woman, you know. Very ill. And Doctor Burleigh wants to shut me up in an asylum. Do you know what an asylum is, child? It's where they put mad people. Yes, Doctor Burleigh wants to send me to a mad-house. He thinks I'm a maniac. But I'm not! Oh dear, no! I'm only ill . . . under-nourished. I must have a special diet, dear child."

While she was speaking the old woman had slithered her great body along the sofa until she sat next to her grand-daughter. She stroked her hair, ran her hands over the girl's shoulders, caressed her neck.

"You love your old grandmother, don't you, Mary?"

"Yes." Mary felt uncomfortable. Granny looked so strange—almost as if she *were* mad.

Mrs. Hinton got up and went over to the door. The key was in the lock. She turned it, and, slipping it into her work-bag, returned to the sofa.

"We must be quick, my dear, if you really wish to help your granny. They'll be back soon—Charteris and that McBride."

"What is it you want me to do?"

"Just give me a little present . . . something I need, something . . ." she almost spat out the words, ". . . something I must have."

"Don't, Granny," Mary laughed nervously, "you're frightening me."

"There's no need to be frightened. I don't want much. Just a cupful. One teacupful of your young healthy blood. You'd give that to make your Granny well again, wouldn't you, Mary?"

"Don't say things like that . . . I'm going. Let me out."

"Don't be a silly little girl. I'm not going to hurt you. I'll let you out when you've given me your little present."

The child started to cry.

"Now there's no need to cry, dear. Come along, there's no time to waste."

With incredible speed for her bulk, Mrs. Hinton lumbered to the tea-table and picked up a table-knife that lay there. Wide-eyed with terror Mary watched her. Then she screamed. Like a tigress the woman turned, her face distorted with rage and fear.

"Stop it, you silly child. Stop it or I'll cut your throat."

Blinded by her tears, and half choked by sobs and fear, the little girl ran to the door, rattling the knob and shaking it with all the sum of her small strength. But in a flash the old woman was after her. Mary felt her grandmother's hand on her neck, wrenching her from her hold. Propelled by a last powerful push the child staggered back to the sofa. With deadly purpose Mrs. Hinton was upon her, the knife in her hand.

"Mummy! . . . Mummy! . . . Nurse Charteris . . . help. . . ."

She pushed the child's head back, until the throat was taut.

Meanwhile Nurse Charteris picked up the telephone.

"Yes?"

"Is that Nurse Charteris?"

"Speaking."

"This is Doctor Burleigh. I rang you up to tell you that . . ."

Suddenly the line was disconnected. Nurse Charteris bounced the hook on the instrument up and down. She felt very vexed. Really the operators were getting worse and worse.

"Exchange! . . . Exchange! I've been cut off!"

"Kaindly replace your receiver and I'll call you again," came the refined tones of the operator.

Nurse Charteris obeyed these instructions with bad grace, and stood waiting, impatiently tapping the floor with her shoe. She wondered uneasily, if she had done wrong in leaving Mrs. Hinton

—but she could hardly get into any trouble in the short time she would be away.

She looked with displeasure at the telephone. After three minutes the bell rang again. Nurse Charteris picked it up, clucking with annoyance.

"Nurse Charteris? We were cut off. I rang you up to tell you to give Mrs. Hinton a sedative so that she will have a good night before her move. You'd better give medinol. What? Yes, the same as before. I'll come round in the morning before she leaves. Good-bye."

Nurse Charteris heard the click of the receiver as the line went dead.

The telephone was on a table that stood in a corner under the staircase. Nurse Charteris thought that since she was downstairs she might as well have a word with Mrs. Willoughby about the final preparations. She found her employer in the drawing-room, sunk in a deep chair, a book in her hand. Nurse Charteris glanced at the room with appreciation. So quiet and restful, with its discreet lighting and crackling wood fire!

"You want me, Nurse?"

"I just looked in to ask if there was anything you wished to see me about."

"No. I think everything is arranged. Doctor Burleigh is coming in the morning, half an hour before the ambulance." She laid down her book. "Oh, Nurse, I know we are doing the right thing; but somehow it seems awful!"

"You've done all you can for your mother," she answered, trim and capable in her severe uniform.

Joan smiled sadly in agreement, and then added: "I suppose we all have. Will you ask Thompson to come here, on your way up."

Nurse Charteris walked briskly to the pantry, delivered her message, and preceded him down the passage to the hall. As they passed the drawing-room, they heard Mary's scream; stifled and far away. There was terror in that cry—and it came from above, from Mrs. Hinton's room. And why had it ended so abruptly? She put her hand on Thompson's arm—"Good God! That child's gone up there . . . it's Mrs. Hinton! I may need your help."

She ran up the stairs, the man following. As she turned the

corner she caught a glimpse of Joan's face of startled inquiry below her. She ran to Mrs. Hinton's room, her arm outstretched for the handle. It was locked. She realised that she must keep calm.

"Mrs. Hinton! Open the door, please. It's Nurse Charteris."

There was no answer. The silence in the room was intense, unnatural . . . and someone waited and listened.

"Mrs. Hinton! Open the door at once. I know you're there." Impatiently she rattled the knob.

From inside the room she heard a low groan. Her eyes narrowed. Mary was hurt. God only knew what that old devil had done to her. She looked at Thompson's broad shoulders. Yes, he would make short work of the door.

"Mrs. Hinton, if you don't open the door I shall break it down."

This time she heard stealthy movements from the locked room.

Nurse Charteris nodded to Thompson. He threw his weight against the door, which held firm. Again he lunged against it; this time he was rewarded by a protesting creak. Mrs. Willoughby and the parlour-maid, attracted by the noise, hurried down the passage. Thompson stepped back a few paces from the door and then flung himself forward with all his force. There was a sound of splintering wood and it swung open. As they surged into the room Mrs. Hinton twisted round from the object on the sofa that engaged her attention.

While she hesitated on the threshold of the room, Joan's first dazed impression was that the lower half of her mother's face was coloured red, and that she wore red gloves on her hands.

PREMIÈRE

The Majestic Cinema was a blaze of light. The name of the Super Production that was about to have its première winked in giant letters. The luminaries of the silver screen that graced this particular opus were likewise honoured in fiery neon. The pavement in front of the entrance was floodlit—posses of policemen kept free a long gangway to the street to allow the "first nighters" an uninterrupted passage into the theatre. Cameras, mounted on trucks, were trained on the notable arrivals as they stepped from their motor cars and hurried past the crowds of celebrity spotters into the sanctuary of the foyer. The performance was billed to begin at a quarter to nine, but it was already three-quarters of an hour past that time, and still newcomers were pouring into the auditorium. "Seats bookable, 5s. to five guineas," the advance publicity had announced. A few shabbily dressed men were haunting the fringe of the mass of sightseers, hawking tickets that they had had the foresight to purchase with this end in view.

The Mills of God had taken a year to make and had been completed at the staggering figure of two million pounds sterling. The stars of the picture were as numerous as those of heaven. Film history was to be made. The greatest, grandest dramatic spectacle of all time was to be unwound before the wondering gaze of London's élite, who were jostling and pushing their ways in a most unmannerly fashion to the staircases and doorways, that led to their dearly-bought stalls and Royal Circles as society photographers kept up a bewildering bombardment of blinding flashes—attempting to obtain pictures of those who were "news"—and battling valiantly against the wiles of the humbler stratas of the gathering whose wish it was to be so termed. Little knots of friends greeted one another, and stood gossiping of this and of that at strategic points of inconvenience to the intense irritation of the later arrivals who either had not won such advantageous positions for themselves, or who wished to get comfortably settled before the start of the performance.

At the entrance, an immaculate Announcer was broadcasting the list of famous pleasure seekers as they arrived—a custom imported from the United States, and one that was immensely popular with a minority of the people so described.

"The time is now growing short," the young man declared with perfect enunciation, "*The Mills of God* is about to begin! I wish that you could see the brilliant gathering that we have with us at the Majestic Cinema to-night. Lady Juliet Ramsbury has just entered accompanied by Peter Arlington, the noted novelist. . . . Here comes Lord Lundy escorting the glamorous Dolores Denby, famous star of the silent days—I beg your pardon?—Miss Denby wishes me to tell her unseen fans that she loves them all as much as ever. She also wishes me to tell them that she starts work on her first talking-picture *Souls in Pawn* next week . . . and who is this? Miss Lairma Strang, famous Mayfair beauty. She is with her mother, and a young man whose name I don't know—but who looks very proud to be seen with Miss Strang. . . . And here comes Sylvia Panson, starring to-night at the Majestic Cinema in *The Mills of God*—and doesn't she look lovely! She is accompanied by Alex Boronoff, the director of the film. They have come to England especially for this première. As you may know *The Mills of God* took fourteen months to make, cost over ten million dollars and commands the services of eighteen stars of the first magnitude. Five lives were lost in the filming of the Casino Fire sequence. Well, ladies and gentlemen, I must close down now—*The Mills of God* is about to begin."

Gradually the foyer emptied, and only the crowd in the Square outside the theatre held in check by the cordon of police, waited for the film to finish so that they might see again their favourites as they struggled out into the night, having witnessed the first performance in Great Britain of *The Mills of God*.

Half a dozen imposing flunkeys in gorgeous liveries, and with shapely and over-robust legs, lounged in the scented, air-conditioned hall of the Majestic, their duties ended until after midnight.

Mary Gordon was one of the five extras who had been so unlucky as to lose their lives in the filming of the epic production. Together with

*three girls and a young man she had perished in a blazing inferno of ply-
wood and canvas. The end had been swift, inevitable and agonising. She
had known with a dread certainty that her life was over. The disaster
duly shocked the Excelsior Company who, however, made full use of the
resultant publicity.*

*Shortly after the conflagration died down Mary found herself stand-
ing outside the well-known Golden Gates. Saint Peter was kindness
itself to her. He informed her that it was necessary to ask a few questions in accordance with the rules of entry, and Mary fully realised that
it would be useless to tell lies to this benevolent but shrewd old gentleman. Accordingly she gave truthful replies to his queries as to her life,
motives and actions. She was a little astonished to find that her evening
dress which she had been wearing at the time of her death was quite
undamaged by the flames. This pleased her, for, like most of her sex, she
considered first impressions all important.*

*Eventually Saint Peter came to the end of his examination, and
Mary waited for him to let her into the heavenly garden of which she
had a pleasant, if vague, idea—a relic of the early religious teaching
imparted to her by her mother, who had been a devout Scotswoman.*

*"My child," Saint Peter said, "you have done but little with your
opportunities. You have been selfish, thoughtlessly intolerant, and
bitter. But your trials have been many, and you have never wantonly
destroyed the happiness of another. Therefore, before you pass on, will I
give you one earthly wish. Tell me what it is that you would like to pos-
sess before you enter the land of no possessions."*

*Mary looked at him to see if he was sincere. Always having had to
look after herself she suspected trickery.*

"Fame?" she answered with decision.

"Film Fame?" she added to clarify her desire.

*The old man bowed his head in acquiescence. . . . The Golden
Gates grew fainter . . . an utter stillness surrounded her . . . she floated
through illimitable space . . . sinking gently through mist grey and soft
as the smoke of a wood fire seen curling in the still air of a summer's
evening.*

Mary sat in the middle of the second row of the "Royal
Circle." A magnificent chinchilla coat covered her evening dress
of silver brocade. Immediately in front of her were Boronoff and

Sylvia Panson. They had just settled themselves into their seats and Boronoff had relieved his lovely Star of her wrap. They were pleasantly conscious of being the cynosure of all eyes.

The Silly Symphony which preceded the main attraction received the usual enthusiastic reception, then, with deep and significant preliminary chords, the words *The Mills of God* in ragged letters caused a murmur of anticipation.

On Mary's right was a good-looking young man. He was smoking a cigar, and while the list of players occupied the attention of his companion he leaned across Mary, with what she considered a marked lack of courtesy, and addressed himself to the girl on her left; remarking that "Micky could have come after all. One can usually find a single seat even on the night itself." He then arranged himself in greater comfort and prepared to enjoy Excelsior's latest offering. Mary felt that she had no existence whatsoever, and registered the impression that the English were just as offhand as she had always imagined.

And now the film had begun. For a time nothing untoward occurred. Gary Trent who played the hero, made his first appearance. Mary waited. A ballroom scene followed in which she had participated. She scanned the crowd of dancers but was unable to identify herself. And here was Sylvia, timing a beautifully planned entrance. But not alone as had been scheduled, for beside her, mimicking her gestures to burlesque, stepped and grimaced Mary Gordon. There was a moment of surprised silence followed by a roar of appreciative laughter. Everything that the star did—the silent shadow ridiculed. Trent, apparently unaware that his heroine was labouring under great dramatic difficulties, never batted an eyelid. Never had there been such a comedy team— never such direction! The audience was delighted and bellowed their appreciation. Sylvia Panson was horrified. She glanced at Boronoff, for an explanation of this outrage. She could hardly believe her eyes. What was this posturing impudent creature she saw on the screen?

Boronoff, his face absolutely expressionless, was hypnotised by the extraordinary occurrence. Fingering the black pearls in the stiff expanse of his shirt front he did not dare to look at Sylvia. He must have gone nuts, he thought despairingly. And still the audience laughed; laughed until they cried, until they were exhausted and could laugh no more.

Before the end of the performance Sylvia and Alex left without speaking a word to anyone. Like sleepwalkers they found their car; oblivious of the crowd of patient admirers; forgetful of the minor Royalty who wished them to be presented, of the high representatives of Excelsior Films—of everyone and of everything.

"We must not refer to this thing—even to each other," they told themselves. "That is the only way to preserve our sanity."

The morning papers were ecstatic. *The Mills of God* instead of occupying the film section of the Dailies concerned, sprang on to the front pages. Not a single voice was raised in disagreement that Excelsior had given birth to the greatest laugh provoker that had yet been made.

Boronoff blinked in amazement at the heap of newspapers stacked on the table in his sitting-room at the Ritz-Splendide. His hair was tousled. He had not troubled to change his clothes from the night before. His shirt was crumpled and soiled—his tie a draggled memory of the dapper white bow of the previous evening. Gingerly he sorted the pile of newsprint.

CHARLIE CHAPLIN MUST LOOK TO HIS LAURELS was how the *Sun* headed its notice.

GREATEST COMEDIENNE THE SCREEN HAS YET GIVEN TO US enthused the *Planet*.

ANONYMOUS STAR STEALS PICTURE announced the *Londoner*.

BORONOFF FOOLS THE PUBLIC—AND THE PUBLIC LIKES IT! was how the *News* reacted.

EXCELSIOR'S NEW DISCOVERY A GENIUS said the *Rocket*.

On no previous occasion had a première caused such a stir— never before had a film received such an ovation!

As a man in a trance Boronoff let the papers fall to the carpet. He looked at his watch. It was nearly eight o'clock. He turned, and for a long time he studied his face in the mirror of the door.

The telephone shrilled but he paid no attention. It continued to ring throughout the day. Reporters, competitors, friends —calls from Paris—New York—Hollywood. Telegrams, cables, notes by messenger boys. At nine o'clock, Hilby, Alex's secretary, arrived to deal with them. He, too, had been at the performance. One look at his employer and he asked no questions. The great director was a broken man!

Mary Gordon once again stood before the Golden Gates. As at their first meeting the old gentleman was there to greet her.

"Well, my dear?"

Mary smiled at him, her eyes shining with gratitude. "And to think," *she said, "I never thought of comedy!"*

Saint Peter stood aside to let her pass through into the promised land.

Crowds besieged the Majestic Cinema after papers had made their appearance. In some inexplicable way the news of a mystery had become common knowledge. The theatre was packed, and long queues stretched for a mile outside the doors. Mounted policemen assisted their pedestrian comrades to control the traffic and to keep the peace.

The extraordinary occurrence was never solved—for after that first performance, the film was shown exactly as it had been made. No silent comedienne convulsed packed houses with her antics.

But the Press became very unpopular. The public does not like being hoaxed.

ANGELA

She was very slim and tall in her blue working overall, her hands covered in thick gloves of greenish rubber. The evening of the late June day flooded the studio with colour catching the glints of the acid-filled pans, purple and malachite, and the pure flame of sun on clear water. She arranged the prints that she carried to dry—the last of the batch—and picked up the list that lay on the small workmanlike desk. This was a formidable one marked "urgent." She checked the names that scaled the long ruled page.

"For Wednesday—without fail." James Hudson. Mrs. Charles Halkin. Sir Harold Keen. The Onyx Car Company. Lady Bridgett Roads. Professor Nicoskoff. "Thursday." Joan Rawlings. Xandra Milton . . . and so through that week and the two that followed.

"Photographs by 'Jera.' "

Her individualist style, love of beauty and talent for the dramatic, had won her a front place in the ranks of fashionable photographers, so that at the age of twenty-eight her annual income was in the region of three thousand a year.

The telephone started its dual summons. Jill picked up the receiver. "Yes? This is the studio. What name do you say? No. I'm afraid Friday is the earliest possible moment."

She went to speak to the two young men who worked in the developing-room, untidy and expert, with chemical-stained fingers.

"Coventry, I'm afraid I shall want you and Hamblen to work overtime for the next few days. I'm sorry, but things may begin to slacken off next month."

"That's quite all right, Miss Grey."

Later in the evening the effects of her work began to tell on Jill. She was glad that she was not dining out, and that John was coming to dine in the flat with Angela and herself. She sat on the soft chintz-covered stool before the triple looking-glass and studied her face. Large grey eyes set a little obliquely in her head, a wide mouth, short nose and pale skin peppered with freckles.

Her friends had likened her to a faun with her tiny pointed ears and wind-blown hair. A face that arrested attention first, and fascinated later. She was looking tired, Jill thought, and almost automatically began to rub a little colour into her cheeks to distract attention from the bruised shadows under her eyes. Her expression, which until now had been intent on the matter in hand, altered. Life seemed to die. What difference could it make to John if she looked tired or not. It was her voice she must keep fresh. He was quick to notice changes in her voice and in her step. She supposed that blindness sharpened one's other faculties, at least so she had always been told. She considered the photograph on her dressing-table and remembered the struggle she had had with John at the sitting. He had laughed at her ideas and would not be serious; had burlesqued the attitudes which she had suggested, and at length had become angry and had said that she must take him as he was and no poodle-faking cinema stuff. She had taken his photograph at that moment, and the handsome petulant face was the more vital for the spontaneous drama. Still holding the rouge she studied the print with its strong black and white lighting, the head half-turned over the broad shoulder. She heard a knock at the door and Mrs. Walters, the feminine half of the married couple that ran the flat, came in. Mrs. Walters was that uncommon being, a "treasure." The daughter of a butler whose family had for generations been in service, she had married, just after the War, an ex-batman, to whom she was devoted. While not approaching her in efficiency, nevertheless he carried out his duties adequately, and the flat, as far as Jill was concerned, ran itself; despite the well-meaning if ineffectual efforts of Angela to fill in her day with attempted supervision.

"Mr. Lang is here, miss."

"Tell him I'll be ready in a minute—oh, and Mrs. Walters, give him a drink."

She hadn't realised that it was so late; and John hated to be kept waiting.

He was standing by the fire when Jill entered, holding a whisky and soda.

"I'm sorry not to have been ready when you arrived, darling, but there is so much to do in the studio just now, and I hurried as much as I could."

"Still minting money! Selfishly, Jill, I hate to think of your working so hard when there is so little I can do to help."

There was no complaint in his voice, only a drear acceptance of his infirmity. "Sometimes," he continued, "I think I should learn to plait those wicker mats that can be sold at three times their value by charitable persons. I might even make a pound a week with which to help support my wife."

"Don't, John. Stop it, please."

"I'm sorry, Jill. Don't pay any attention to me. Self-pity is a luxury that few of us can afford."

They sat in silence for some minutes. The room was so quiet that the rustle of the logs as they settled in the ash whispered very distinctly. Angela bustled into the room, over-feminine in her dinner dress of frilled chiffon.

"Hello, John." She spoke with what seemed to the man as infuriating tenderness. "Dinner's ready. Take my arm."

Jill winced for him, knowing well how he disliked needless assistance.

"I can manage all right, Angela, thank you all the same." He stood up, waiting for the two women to precede him to the dining-room. During dinner Angela said that Romaine Deering, a great friend of hers, and an industrious, if ineffectual, novelist of the romantic school, was calling for her and that they were going to see a Russian film entitled "Avarice" at one of the highly selective cinemas in the region of the Adelphi. She had pseudo-intellectual interests. Oddly enough John was an enthusiastic filmgoer, and found it amusing to try and piece together the story from the dialogue and sound effects, afterwards checking up his ideas with Jill.

They were both relieved to hear that Angela was going out that evening, and, as soon as the door had closed behind the backs of the two "fans," for Romaine had arrived punctually to pick her up, the peaceful atmosphere with which Jill had so effortlessly imbued the flat, began to have a soothing effect on John's dangerously raw nerves.

"Poor Angela!" Jill said. "Fortunately she is oblivious of her powers of irritation. John, I've been wondering . . . do you think

I could suggest that I should take a small flat for her after we're married?"

He did not reply. Jill glanced at him quickly. "John, do you?"

"After we're married?" He spoke with sudden vehemence. "Jill, you can't tie yourself to me. In a few years I'll be a neurotic wreck. I've not the stuff of heroes."

Jill stared into the fire. She sat on a tweed-covered tuffet, her head against his knee.

"I see no point in waiting, darling. We'll both be much happier, I know. Let's be married next month."

John made no answer, but leant down and kissed her hungrily, in panic that he should lose all that he loved in his dark bewildering world.

Angela was unable to sleep. All through the night she was in that unenviable state of semi-consciousness in which troubles seem insuperable and a burning feeling of injustice consumes the hapless victim. She lay now considering the question of Jill's attitude towards John. She did not consider that her sister treated him with the thoughtfulness to which his affliction entitled him. How unfair it was that Jill did not appreciate the trust that had been given her. Why, at times she was even brusque with the poor boy . . . so helpless—and once so strong. Angela lay staring into the gloom considering the unfairness of the world. She had not got very much out of her forty years of life. Somewhere a clock muffled by the distance struck five times.

It was after nine when she awoke, and, struggling into her dressing-gown, padded into Jill's room. She found her dressed and about to start for her work. Mrs. Walters waited at her elbow. Jill handed a pad back to her. "Yes, that will do very nicely. I shall dine out to-night, but Miss Angela will be in . . . won't you?" she added, turning to her sister.

"Yes. I thought perhaps I would ask Romaine to dine if she is free."

"Of course. Mrs. Walters, is Beckwith ready?"

"Yes, miss. The car was here five minutes ago."

Jill shut the door of the flat behind her and pressed the button of the lift. She stepped out into the sunny street, a feeling of well-being in her heart.

Beckwith sprang forward.

"Good morning, miss."

"Good morning."

The curves of strong leather on his burly calves flashed in the sunlight.

"I'm a little late I think. Is it a quarter-past yet?"

His hand fumbled underneath his coat. "Nearly twenty-past, miss."

"Go straight to the studio, please."

The car moved off. From her bedroom window Angela watched it go. Funny how servants adored Jill. She considered at times that Jill was a shade too familiar with him. Beckwith was good-looking. A pity that he was her sister's chauffeur. . . .

Jill came back early to change, as she was going to a play, and Angela talked to her while she was having her bath. Small criticisms and complaints, and pathetic, unimportant confidences. Jill, wrapped in a towel of thick fleece and of gigantic dimensions, interrupted her once to say:

"John knows I'm dining out to-night—but should he forget and telephone, tell him I'll be back before twelve if he wants to talk to me."

After she had gone, Angela settled herself with a book to await Romaine's arrival. She was finishing the first chapter when the telephone shrilled.

"Yes? . . . Yes, it's Angela speaking . . . really, Romaine, I must say I think it's most inconsiderate of you . . . no, I'm afraid not . . . but that's quite all right." Her lips were pursed into a tight bud of pique and disappointment. "No, dear, of course I don't. . . . Yes, I quite understand. . . . I don't exactly know. . . . I'm rather busy this week as a matter of fact. Good-bye, dear." She replaced the receiver briskly. She crossed to the bell. While she waited she lit a cigarette.

"Mrs. Walters . . . I shall be alone for dinner to-night." Once again the telephone clamoured for attention. The housekeeper moved to answer it.

"Hello . . . yes? . . ." She turned to Angela. "It's Mr. John."

"Tell him I'll speak to him."

"One moment, sir."

Angela hurried across the room.

"Hello . . . John?"

"That you, Angela? Jill out?"

"Yes . . . didn't she tell you she was going to the theatre?"

"I believe she did . . . well, good-bye, Angela. What time will she be back?"

"Before twelve, she said. One minute, John, why don't you come and dine with me? There's plenty of food, as Romaine had to cry off at the last minute."

There was a short pause. John thought, 'Poor Angela—she's lonely and unhappy.'

"Yes—I'd like to dine."

The line went dead. Angela told Mrs. Walters of this re-arrangement of her plans and returned to her bedroom to change her dress for a suit of satin pyjamas—blue velvet with gold embroidery. She was ready as the doorbell rang. Snatching up her bag she was reclining gracefully on the sofa when John was shown in. It was only then that she realised how unnecessary these preparations had been. "Still," she comforted herself, "it makes me feel more assured, even if John can't appreciate it."

"Angela—my eyes hurt a little to-night—it was the heat from the streets, I think. I wonder if you'd find me the eye lotion that Jill keeps for me. I think it's in the cupboard in the bathroom."

Dinner was over and they were back in the drawing-room drinking coffee.

"Of course." Angela got up and went in search of the lotion, returning a minute later holding it in her hand with a swab of lint. He turned his face to her. She noticed the lids of his eyes seemed inflamed. Gently she bathed them with the soothing liquid.

"That better, John?"

"Yes . . . that's . . . better."

The tension round his mouth relaxed. Angela's eyes tear-dimmed as she rested her hand on his shoulder.

"Poor old boy," she whispered.

"You're kind, Angela . . . but please, please, don't pity me."

After a while he asked, "What time is it?"

"Half-past ten. Jill will be back in an hour."

"I want to talk to you, Angela . . . about Jill, I mean."

"Yes?" She waited for him to continue.

"Do you think it would be fair to her to let her marry me? She's so wonderful, so clever and so loyal."

"That's rather for you to decide, isn't it?"

"Do you think she loves me?"

Angela made no reply. Suddenly all the jealousy, the loneliness, the bitterness in her soul welled up in a spurt of vicious hatred. John had appeared to have liked being with her, Angela, this evening. She could make him as happy as Jill could, and there were other men who were, or would be, in love with her sister.

"Angela . . . why don't you answer?" He turned towards her inquiringly.

"I don't want you to ask me that question."

"You mean that she doesn't?" He got to his feet and came towards her. In his haste he knocked against a chair. Usually, in a room that he knew, he remembered the exact positions of the furniture. An ashtray on the arm fell to the floor.

"John, please. I'd rather not say."

"You must."

"Then I'm afraid that she doesn't. She's terribly fond of you for all the memories you have together, for what you were before . . . before . . ."

"I went blind. Yes, of course. I understand."

"You won't say anything to Jill, will you?"

"How could I? There's someone else, I suppose?"

"Yes."

"Anyone I know?"

"Jill has such a wide acquaintance."

"But anyone in particular?" he insisted.

"I'm afraid so. Guy Challoner. He's married—but separated from his wife, and of course he's very rich."

"What? I don't believe you. Shut up, do you hear me! You're lying . . . lying . . . I believe that you hate Jill . . . why do you *hate* her so? . . . Yes, I can hear it in your voice. I'm going now . . . you're a filthy liar. . . ." He groped towards the door. At that moment he heard the sound of Jill's latch-key.

Angela tried hard to convince herself that the last few minutes had never happened. She felt herself to be in a vacuum of unreasoning fury and fear.

"Very well. Don't believe it. Perhaps that would be best. You're a fool, John; you're blind in more senses than one."

She found herself in her bedroom behind a locked door. She hated herself. Why, oh, why had she done it? Other people had such simple happy lives. The tears came, salt and painful.

"Hello, John, I'm earlier than I planned to be. We didn't go to a play after all. I came back because I thought that you might be here."

Jill had seen at once that something had occurred, but thought it best to let him take his time. "What have you been doing?" She slipped off her coat and smoothed her hair in the looking-glass.

"I . . . I dined here with Angela."

"How very sweet of you." She picked up a cigarette.

"Jill, be careful, Angela hates you."

The match she was holding flamed until it burned her fingers.

"John—what do you mean?"

"I don't know. I'm tired, Jill. I'm going. Good night, my dear."

"I'll send you back."

"Don't bother, I'll get a taxi."

"Nonsense. Beckwith's still here."

On his way to Travers Square, John's brain was in turmoil. There could be nothing in Angela's horrible accusation, he knew, but supposing Jill still kept up a pretence of loving him . . . far better to break it up . . . finish it all. . . .

Jill knocked at Angela's door, tried the knob. No answer. With a sigh of exasperation she went to her own bedroom.

She was conscious during the weeks that followed of a sense of strain when she was alone with John. He appeared to be listening more acutely, followed her with his seeking sightless face when she left his side, rang her up at all hours during her work. He seemed, too, to rely upon her more exactingly, to hold her arm even when in familiar surroundings, demanded continually to have his eyes bathed, his cigarettes lighted.

One afternoon on her return from luncheon she found Angela waiting for her in the studio.

"You're busy, dear, I know. But I realised this morning that I had never really understood your elaborate job and I just thought I'd like you to take me round."

Jill wasted a precious hour showing her the complicated apparatus of the modern photographer. The elaborate lights, screens, developing and touching-up that the print requires. Several times during the tour of inspection she was called away to urgent telephone conversations. On such times she found her sister engaged in chatting to the assistants, taking an interest in the various processes in which they were engaged.

August came with the oppressive heat that permeates from metalled road surfaces in big cities. Her work was slackening off and Jill was looking forward to the brief holiday in Biarritz that she was taking at the end of the month.

John was waiting for her when she arrived at the flat. She was glad to see him. Lately they had seemed closer than they had been during the spring and early summer. He kissed her, and her eyes closed, and, as he held her tightly in his arms, her mind went back to the man of three years before. Laughing, on the tennis court, the winner of a close set 10–8 with Danios the Spanish champion; shooting in disgracefully shabby tweeds in Scotland; driving her Packhard far too quickly round the dangerous curves of the roads in North Wales.

His hold tightened. "Darling, you were right, we can't do without each other, can we?" He spoke gruffly. "We'll be married right away and go to Biarritz for our honeymoon."

She stroked his thick fair hair, her mouth answering his. At last he drew away.

"My Lord, we've been fools, Jill. The time, the precious time, we've wasted."

She noticed his forehead puckered, as it always was when he was suffering. Even at this time of the day heat was insufferable. "Darling—your eyes are hurting. I'll get your lotion."

"They are rather sore, Jill, darling. That's what I came here to-day to tell you. I saw Elwes last night, and he told me there was a possibility that my sight might come back. He says my eyes are responding to the treatment he's giving me. It will take some time naturally, but in a year or eighteen months if the improvement continues I shall be able to see with the help of spectacles. I'll be able to see again, darling. Think of it . . . to see you and the sky and the green grass. . . ."

"John—how perfectly wonderful! I'm certain you'll be cured. I've always thought so. Doctors never give false encouragement." Jill flung her arms round his neck. "Now, darling, you wait there."

She noticed that the green bottle was almost empty, but there was another full one placed slightly in front of it. She blessed Mrs. Walters for her efficiency. She took it down and soaked a wad of lint in its contents.

John was sitting on a low stool facing the window. She had forgotten to remove her gloves, but she remembered that witch-hazel did not stain. Carefully she bathed his eyes, pressed the healing swab firmly on to the inflamed lids. The muscles round John's mouth tightened, quivered as if he were enduring great pain. Then, against his control, dreadful choking moans filled the room. Horrified, Jill dropped the bottle on the white carpet.

"Jill—what have you done? Christ—it hurts . . . it *hurts*. . . ." His hands clawed at his face, tearing at his eye-sockets.

"Darling . . . John, what is it?"

She looked at the bottle on the floor. The contents had spilled on to the carpet, eroding the fabric. Her gloves, too, were turning black. She tore them off.

"God help me!"

John was by the window, his knees against the low sill, arms upflung to protect his face. Jill ran towards him. Unthinkingly, with the instinct of a hurt animal, he stepped back, staggered and crashed down to the street below. Jill stood quite still, momentarily paralysed with horror. Then she screamed.

"Angela . . . Mrs. Walters . . . Mrs. Walters . . . *Mrs. Walters*. . . ."

Footsteps ran towards the drawing-room. In their hurry the two women hustled each other in the doorway.

"Look at the carpet . . . look. . . ."

The acid had burned through to the wood.

"Never mind, miss, don't take on so," Mrs. Walters comforted. "We can have a new piece let in."

"But the bottle . . . John's eye-lotion."

"I think you must have taken the wrong bottle, Jill," Angela broke in. "That was a bottle of acid one of your men gave me. He said it would take the stains off the wash-basin in my bedroom. Stupid of me to have left it in your cupboard when I had put it in one of John's empty bottles of eye lotion. But I don't see there's any need to make such a fuss. I'm sorry, I'm sure."

She looked at Jill with an expression very near to tranquillity. . . . "Really, it wasn't my fault. Accidents will happen as everybody knows."

Wide-eyed, Jill looked at her. Roughly she pushed past them and ran out of the flat, and the lift doors clanged behind her.